THE HUMAN COUNTRY:
NEW AND COLLECTED STORIES

Works by Harry Mathews

FICTION
The Conversions
Tlooth
Country Cooking and Other Stories
The Sinking of Odradek Stadium
Cigarettes
Singular Pleasures
The American Experience
The Journalist
Sainte Catherine
The Human Country: New and Collected Stories

POETRY
The Ring: Poems 1956-1969
The Planisphere
Trial Impressions
Le Savior des rois
Armenian Papers: Poems 1954-1984
Out of Bounds
A Mid-Season Sky: Poems 1954-1991
Alphabet Gourmand (with Paul Fournel)

MISCELLANIES
Selected Declarations of Dependence
The Way Home: Selected Longer Prose
Écrits français

NONFICTION AND CRITICISM
The Orchard: Remembrance of Georges Perec
20 Lines a Day
Immeasurable Distances: The Collected Essays
Giandomenico Tiepolo
Oulipo Compendium (with Alastair Brotchie)

The Human Country:
New and Collected Stories

HARRY MATHEWS

Dalkey Archive Press

Copyright © 2002 by Harry Mathews
Drawings in "The Way Home" copyright © 1988 by Trevor Winkfield
First edition, 2002
All rights reserved

"Tradition and the Individual Talent: The 'Bratislava Spiccato,' " "The Dialect of the
Tribe," "The Novel as History," "Country Cooking," "The Network," "Remarks of the
Scholar Graduate," and "The Ledge" first appeared in *Country Cooking and Other Stories*
(Burning Deck, 1980). "Their Words, for You" originally appeared in *Selected Declarations
of Dependence* (Z Press, 1977; Sun & Moon, 1996) and is reprinted here with the
permission of Sun & Moon Press, Los Angeles, CA. "The Way Home" is included in *The
Way Home* (Atlas Press, 1989) and is reprinted here with the permission of Atlas Press,
London. "Journeys to Six Lands" was originally published as a *livre d'artiste* by URDLA
(Lyons), with nine lithographs by Hugh Weiss, and was also published in the *Chicago
Review*. "Tear Sheet," "Letters from Yerevan," "The Chariot," "Franz Kafka in Riga" and
"Still Life" first appeared in *The American Experience* (Atlas Press, 1991). "Dear Mother"
first appeared in *Denver Quarterly*, "Mr. Smathers" in *Murmur*, "Brendan" in *Fourteen Hills
— The SGSU Review*, "The Broadcast" in *Mark's*, "Calibrations of Latitude" in *Boston Review*,
"The Taxidermist" in *New York Sex: Stories* (Painted Leaf Press, 1998), "Soap Opera" in
Press, "Clocking the World on Cue: The Chronogram for 2001" in *Conjunctions*, and "One-
Way Mirror" in *Common Knowledge*.

Library of Congress Cataloging-in-Publication Data:

Mathews, Harry, 1930-
     The human country : new and collected stories / Harry Mathews.-- 1st ed.
        p. cm.
     ISBN 1-56478-321-9 (acid-free paper)
        1. United States--Social life and customs--20th century--Fiction. I. Title.
     PS3563.A8359 H86 2002
     813'.54--dc21

                                                                              2002073509

Partially funded by grants from the Lannan Foundation and the Illinois Arts Council, a
state agency.

Dalkey Archive Press books are published by the Center for Book Culture, a nonprofit
organization with offices in Chicago and Normal, Illinois.

www.centerforbookculture.org

Printed on permanent/durable acid-free paper and bound in the United States of America.

TABLE OF CONTENTS

I. FIRST STORIES

II. THE AMERICAN EXPERIENCE: STORIES TO BE READ ALOUD

III. CALIBRATIONS OF LATITUDE

I

First Stories

TRADITION AND THE INDIVIDUAL TALENT:
THE "BRATISLAVA SPICCATO"

In August 1877 the celebrated conductor Jenö Szenkar, who six weeks earlier had gone to Graz to visit his friend the violinist Benno Bennewitz, and incidentally to perform with him the cycle of the Beethoven violin sonatas, left that city for Budapest, where he was engaged to conduct two operas at the summer festival. This was the Jenö Szenkar whose wife's elder brother was the grandfather of Geza Anda. Benno Bennewitz for his part was Teresa Stich-Randall's maternal great-grandfather, and his niece was Dietrich Fischer-Dieskau's mother. Szenkar's stay in Graz had been motivated not by professional reasons but by concern for his health. The winter in Vienna had become a grueling one, since he not only had been chief conductor at the Staatsoper but had prepared several concerts with the Philharmonic Orchestra: it was in connection with the latter responsibility that he had become involved in bitter public controversy with Ludwig Krumpholz (who, much later, was Hermann Scherchen's godfather) over the performance of the cadenzas in Joseph-Leopold Pitsch's posthumous piano concerto. Pitsch's widow, the following year, was to marry Karl Knappertsbusch and by him bear the father of Hans Knappertsbusch. The unexpected battle with Krumpholz had lessened the benefits brought him by the assistance of young Franz Mittag. (Mittag as an infant had shared a wet nurse with Irmgaard Dehn, for whom her granddaughter Irmgaard Seefried was named.) This was no fault of Mittag: he had done brilliant work, and thanks to the impression he then made he was named only two years later to the directorship of the opera, after a year's interim under the aging Julius Meyer-Remy, the great-grandfather of both Hugo Meyer-Welfing and Mrs. Rudolph Bing. Szenkar had finished the season in a state of exhaustion, and he had dearly counted on his sojourn in Graz to restore him. The concerts with Bennewitz required little exertion — playing the piano was for him a pastime, he loved his fiddler friend, it was the best kind of busman's holiday. His hopes of recovery, however, were disappointed, for he had hardly been in Budapest a week when he died, felled by a stroke during a rehearsal of *Childe Harold*. This now-forgotten opera was by Bela Hubay, whose great-grandson married George Szell's sister.

Szenkar was much loved in Budapest, and although he was taken for burial to his home town of Kaposvar, the city put on a grand memorial service for him. To this event many musicians came from all over Central Europe.

Among them was the Czech violinist Vaclav Czegka. The Czegkas have of course always been a central force in the musical life of their country — Rafael Kubelik is Vaclav Czegka's great-great-nephew. A lifelong friend of Szenkar, of whom he was a little the senior, Czegka undertook the trip to Budapest without hesitation, but not without misgiving, for his own health was frail. Accordingly he sent a telegram to his son Frantisek (who would three years later marry Clara Riemenschneider, the grandmother of Inge Borkh), a musician himself, then touring in Klagenfurt: he should journey at once to Györ, where he would join his father, who would thus not have to travel alone all the way from Brno to Budapest. It should perhaps be mentioned that Czegka had lived by himself since the death of his wife the year before. She had been born a Kalliwoda, a family to which Rudolph Firkusny is related.

During the train ride a certain line of thought that Czegka had been following for many months at last reached its conclusion. It had started at the very performance by Krumpholz of the Pitsch concerto that had given Szenkar such trouble. Through an adroit combination of pedaling and touch Krumpholz had demonstrated a novel effect, that of making the hammers "bounce drily" on the strings. Czegka had then begun wondering whether the violin bow could not produce a similar effect. He had pondered, he had experimented, above all he had discussed the matter daily with his son-in-law, the cellist Jan Ševčík. (Through her remarriage with László Thoman, Ševčík's mother would have a grandson who was second cousin once removed of Ferenc Fricsay and first cousin twice removed of Sandor Vegh.) Before their discussions could bear fruit, Ševčík had left for Ljubljana, where he was engaged to play with Gustav Henschkel (Clemens Krauss's maternal grandfather) and Friedrich Rheinberger. It was on this occasion that Rheinberger met Olga Czerny (no relation), whom he later married and by whom he had several children, none of them musical. Rheinberger's sister, however, was Wolfgang Windgassen's grandmother, and one of his brothers was throughout their school years the best friend of Wolfgang Schneiderhan's father.

It was as his train pulled into the Bratislava station that Vaclav Czegka discovered how the desired "dry bounce" could be realized. Such was his astonishment that he cried out, and under the strain of that cry he felt his old heart falter. He looked around for a confidant to whom, in case the worst happened, he might entrust his secret. No one besides a very old lady shared his compartment. He strode the length of his car but only traveling salesmen, governesses with children, and other hopeless cases were to be seen. Unwisely he leaped from the train onto the station platform, and doing so felt a surge of darkness within him. The platform was empty except for a young rabbi. Czegka staggered toward him, fell on his knees, and managed to gasp out his discovery before his heart quite collapsed.

The rabbi, who had, although he was Russian, a good grasp of German, was Nathan Milstein's father. Returning to Odessa, he repeated what he had learned to a professor at the St. Petersburg Conservatory, Boris Zaremba. (He was the great-uncle both of Boris Khaikin and, through a niece's Bulgarian marriage, Boris Christoff.)

These facts supply a partial explanation of the excellence of Russian violinists in the twentieth century, and clarify the origins of the controversial expression "Bratislava spiccato."

THE DIALECT OF THE TRIBE

for Georges Perec

Thank you for the letter suggesting I contribute to the Festschrift in your honor. I have never doubted that in translating your work I have been of service to our two cultures, but I am flattered to think that my general views on translation may be worth a hearing. I shall be happy to contribute to the homage you are deservedly to receive, not only for the privilege of collaborating in so distinguished an enterprise, but because I truly feel that the subject you have assigned me is a vital one. The longer I live — the longer I write — the stronger becomes my conviction that translation is the paradigm, the exemplar of all writing. To put it another way: it is translation that demonstrates most vividly the yearning for transformation that underlies every act involving speech, that supremely human gift. Of course I am not saying that translation — at least not as I practice it — takes precedence over other modes of writing. On the contrary: it is its modesty that makes it so useful. But while it differs enormously in substance from true writing (like your own), the difference is only one of degree. One might then say that insofar as true writing is a kind of translation, the text from which it works is an infinitely arduous one: nothing less than the universe itself.

By coincidence — only minds poorer than ours would call it accident — I was, as you were writing your letter, engaged in radically extending my knowledge of translation, in a way as appropriate as it was unforeseen.

I had returned for ten days to Fitchwinder University in order to continue my research on the Bactrian controversy. Our old friend Ms. Maxine Moon is still a librarian there; and it was she who brought to my attention the unexpected text that was to occupy me during the rest of my stay. This text was not in Bactrian, it was not about Bactria — in fact it put the Bactrians quite out of my head. It was in, of all things, Pagolak, the speech of a small hill tribe in northern New Guinea; and it had been transcribed for an article in an Australian anthropological journal by one Ernest Botherby (bless him!). It was entitled — by Dr. Botherby perhaps — *Kalo Gap Pagolak,* meaning "magic transformation of Pagolak." Ms. Moon, correctly, "thought it would interest" me. The text, she said, was an account of a method used by the Pagolak-speaking tribe to translate their tongue into the dialects of their neighbors. What was remarkable about this method was that while it produced translations that foreign listeners could understand and accept, it also concealed from them the original meaning of every statement made.

You will understand that once I had heard this much, it was impossible not to want to learn more. To translate successfully and not reveal one's meaning — what could be more paradoxical? What could be more relevant? (Is anything more paradoxical than the act of translation?) The crafty Ms. Moon had me hooked. She whetted my craving with the remark that Pagolak was supposedly simple, with structures I could hope to master quickly, and abetted it by supplying two Pagolak dictionaries, one English, the other Dutch.

Ms. Moon had spoken the truth: the language is, as you will see, accessible enough, and I worked long hours at it. I made such progress as to expect by the end of a week to be able to produce an English rendering of *Kalo Gap Pagolak*. (Need I say that you would have been the first beneficiary of this undertaking?) But there is more to any language than its mechanisms, and inherent in the very utterance of Pagolak was something that kept the roughest translation beyond my grasp.

(The dictionaries turned out to be useless. They had been compiled for traders and had only an arbitrary, mercantile utility. The problem, in any case, was not one of particular words.)

As I became familiar with the text, which was an oral declaration by the *abanika* or "chief word-chief" of the tribe, I began wondering why Dr. Botherby had not himself supplied a translation as part of his article. He had done his other work scrupulously: his commentary was packed with useful information; he had clearly taken great care in transcribing the words of the speaker. Had he, too, encountered some obstacle to Englishing the text? The better I understood *Kalo Gap Pagolak*, the surer I became that Dr. Botherby, like myself, had had no choice except to leave the *abanika's* declaration intact. Was it after all so surprising for a language to resist ordinary procedures of translation when it was itself capable of extraordinary ones? What could be more extraordinary than a method that would allow words to be "understood" by outsiders without having their substance given away? It was true that the *abanika* claimed the power of controlling this method for himself; but I was starting to realize how absurd such a claim might be. For it wasn't only those like the *abanika* who had this power, but every last member of his tribe. The method did not depend on individual decision; it was an integral part of the language itself. No one speaking Pagolak could escape it. No one attempting to penetrate Pagolak could elude it.

In a matter of days I found myself perfectly capable of understanding what the *abanika* was saying and perfectly incapable of repeating it in other terms, whether in English, or French — or Middle Bactrian. The *abanika's* declaration, you see, *was* the very process of transforming language that I expected it to be *about*. It was not an account of the process, it was the process itself. And how can you translate a process? You'd have to render not only words but the spaces between them — like snapshooting the invisible air under the beating wings of flight. An impossibility. All that can be done is describe, suggest, record impressions and effects. That is what Dr. Botherby did for his anthropological colleagues. It is the best I can do for you.

From beginning to end, the *abanika's* words concern the means of bringing about *kalo gap,* the "magic changing," the redirecting of language towards foreign ears in a way that both provides clarity and suppresses translation's customary *raison d'être* — the communication of substantive content. You and I may know that such communication is at best hypothetical, perhaps impossible; that translation may, precisely, exorcise the illusion that substantive content exists at all — but what led a remote New Guinean tribe to such a discovery? Why should it care?

My questions are rhetorical: the *abanika* speaks only of hows, not whys. Let me acquaint you with some of his terms. The hermetic transformation he articulates is associated with the word *nalaman.* More precisely: *nalaman* is the final result of the transformation, while the means of achieving that result is *namele.* As you can see, or better hear, if *"namele"* is to become *"nalaman,"* a redistribution of phonemes must take place. Here is a first demonstration of the "magic of changing," in one of its simplest forms. The words representing these changes *(kalo gap)* sometimes involve *namele* and sometimes *nalaman*, according to whether the means or the end is invoked.

Now if *kalo gap* is embodied willy-nilly in the act of speaking Pagolak, awareness of it is something that has to be learned. Young males are schooled in this awareness during their initiation into manhood, or *nuselek*. Dr. Botherby, who underwent the initiation rite *(nanmana)* so as to witness and record it, says that pain and privation make initiates highly receptive, so that they master *namele* rapidly. The core of the instruction *(afanu)* is *sitokap utu sisi*. This phrase leaves an impression, approximately, of "resettling words in [own] eggs": aptly enough, after the youngsters emerge from *afanu* through *sitokap utu sisi* into *nuselek* and its attendant privileges of *ton wusi* and *aban metse,* they claim to be emerging from boyhood (rather: "boybeing") like seabirds from chicken eggs *(utopani inul ekasese nuselek ne sami sisinam)* — dear Christ, it doesn't *mean* that — but can you perhaps intuit how *tokkele* (not "words," *those* words) return to their *sisi* to re-emerge in unexpected, unrecognizable forms?

Sitokap utu sisi — this will surprise no one familiar with the ancient Mysteries, the Kabbala, or modern linguistics — *sitokap utu sisi* requires *sutu* (you cannot call it death — perhaps dying, the dying . . .), *narakaviri* (like fire, like burning — fire-as-burning), and *kot* (not just s--t, but life tumultuously swarming out of the tropical dung, or words to that effect). The crux is *narakaviri*. The *abanika* makes this deafeningly clear as he cries over and over *nuselek ka namele nanmana nalaman nanasiluvo narakaviri* — of course he is, as well, making a magical pun, magical in the incantatory repetition of the initial *na*, punning in that it identifies the initiation of the young men *(nanmana)* with the transformation of language they are submitting to *(namele)*. *Narakaviri ne se eleman* again indicates the primordial role of fire-being-burning, although *sutu* and *kot* are never forgotten. (Examples: *umanisi suta kalasaviri nekkolim* and *tuku kot, kot kotavan*.) But the moment of *narakaviri* is supreme — above all for us, for you and me, writer and translator. *Nusu tese alukan,* you might say (but they would not say it, not in *nalaman,* because *alukan* is a foreign word, meaning "gold").

Now, dear colleague, and companion, please look hard at these two short passages in Pagolak. Each points to *narakaviri,* to this critical moment in *namele.* The first enacts the way up to it *(pakanu),* and the second the way down from it *(plot).* You can enter these passages. What I propose is not reasonable, not unreasonable. Enter these two passages. You have no need for more knowledge. Your awareness is equal to the task. This is a task: like all tasks correctly performed, it leads to revelation. Move (as I did) through the first passage to the last, become the bodily metamorphosis that this movement inspires, and you will have made the great lurch forward in your *afanu.* Then we shall walk in the light of *nuselek* together.

What you must provide is attention. Your attention must be absolutely ready. More than that: you must expand it in a decorum of complete accessibility, in a ripeness as for dying, with the sense of a purpose vast but as yet unknown. Do not think, do not care: Be!

First, *pakanu:*

"Amak esodupelu mukesa dap alemok use dup ulemaka." (Repeat three times.)

Last, *plot:*

"Amak esudupelu moke sadapalemuk use dup olemaka." (Ditto.)

Helpful hints: don't bother with *amak,* a conventional opening

lan; or with *dup,* which signals that an utterance is almost *nalaman.*
Mukesa dap alemok includes, in a polysemistic context, the proverb
"Like jug, cork woman['s mouth]," while *moke sadapalemuk* among
other things refers to a folksong in which "impetuous [husband] with-
draws-from-vagina." (Women are thought to create *namele* naturally,
along with language; but as I hardly need tell you, they have no
mastery of it — no power of *nalaman.*) Similarly, where *use ulemaka*
involves "burning the old field," *use olemaka* leads to "burning (i.e.
cooking) new fish."

Submit to the passages once again. Do you see how beautiful
this is? How brightly *narakaviri* colors the dawn sky? Brighter than
any *ulemaka!* And now how bright and clear it must be that *namele*
never be explained, or *nalaman* understood! Listen: *awa nuselek kot
tak nalaman namele Pagolak!* I promise to steal the book for you, from
this selfsame library — fuck Ms. Moon, since she won't let me Xerox
it. I shall do this for you — what wouldn't I do for you? And even
before you share the totality of the words, you — *abanika* yourself,
abanika esolunava — can partake of my *tunaga* (joy-as-it-becomes-
joy), my utter *nasavuloniputitupinoluvasan,* as the birth-wording goes,
when *alemok* brings forth *tupinohi* who will some day come to *nuselek.*
Such twenty-one carat *alukan* for our own *namele* and *nalaman* —
words into words, sparse scraps resurrected in the plenitude of
unentrammelled recreation! And I promise to turn to the composition for your Festschrift as soon as this letter is mailed. Meanwhile,
*nasavuloniputitupinoluvasan! And let me on this private occasion add a few
last words, spoken out of the fullness of my mind and heart with admiration,
with devotion, with love:* Amak kalo gap eleman nama la n'kat tokkele
sunawa setan amnan umanisi sutu pakotisovulisanan unafat up lenumo
kona kafe avanu lo se akina ba nasavuloniputitupinoluvasan (!!) abanika

esolunava efaka nok omunel put afanu nanasiluvo sitokap utu sisi namu nanmana tes awa nuselek kot tak nalaman namele Pagolak kama —

THE NOVEL AS HISTORY

Robinson was seated in front of the fire.

"I knew Johns," he said. "I met him in Detroit in '38. We were trapped together in a bar by the great blizzard of that winter. It was the only time he ever spoke to me of his past life — of his adventures as sailor and shepherd, of the extraordinary enterprises he had founded in various parts of the world, and of that encounter with Rouxinol you just mentioned, when he lay sick with yellow fever in New Guinea. Rouxinol's devoted care of him, he told me, expressed the silent acknowledgement of a moral debt that the old man had contracted twenty-odd years before: first alpinist to accost the Himalayas, he too had been succored in the helpless aftermath of a solitary fall by one he did not know — Borgmann, the Danish lepidopterist.

"At the time he saved Rouxinol's life, Borgmann was traveling with old Jeremiah Keats, who is best remembered as having been confidential secretary to Kuromato, the original Japanese ambassador to St. Petersburg. The fact has eclipsed his earlier and remarkably versatile career as diplomat and man of letters — Keats was, for instance, instrumental in persuading Ketchum, who until then, using the pen name 'Clarissa Rivers,' had achieved only a mild notoriety as an author of sentimental novels, to leave England and come to Chile. Of course it was in Santiago that Ketchum met Bechstein, the 'nurse at Waterloo' of the historical classic of that name. Bechstein deserved more credit for the book than Ketchum gave him — despite his low rank he was a knowledgeable man, and in his youth he even earned a reputation as a debater in the *Club des Crachats,* the political group that gathered in Paris around the Swiss merchant Willi in the decades before the revolution of '89. Willi may, however, be better known to you as the man who brought the great castrato Pietrini to London to perform in the premiere of Handel's *Acis and Galatea;* it was he furthermore who, much earlier, discovered the incomparable Moroccan weaver el-Saadi and enrolled him in the workshops of Brussels, where he collaborated on the Wagner funerary tapestries now in the Louvre.

"The Wagner so honored had been burgomaster of Lübeck; the salient incident of his life was the fathering of Rosanna Wagner, 'pearl of the Hanse,' whom the Swedish divine Blekinge married in the closing years of the previous century — an event that caused a scandal, and one that was hardly lessened by the disparity between the groom's ninety years and Rosanna's nineteen. Yet Blekinge's initiative was hardly astonishing: he had come late to the cloth, and his career had been fraught with worldly doings. His gallantries are mentioned in the diaries of Cabot, the Majorcan author who, in spite of his foreign birth, distinguished himself among the *précieux* at the French court. It was this very man to whom we owe our knowledge about the advent of the tomato in Burgundian cuisine: he recounts the pioneering work of the Milanese cook Alabastro in Dijon some forty years earlier, at the end of a career that had taken him as far from home as Seville and London. Cabot reports that in his London days Alabastro, then a strikingly beautiful young man, appeared on the stage in female roles under the name of 'J. Pepper.' He would thus have been the original Ophelia; but this is hardly credible, since there are several accounts ascertaining that J. Pepper was the native-born protégé and paramour of Morral, the aging Aragonese whose introduction in an earlier generation of the male curtsey to the court of the Kingdom of Naples set an international fashion.

"A curious element in this history is that Morral had been educated by the stern Protestant Clodius (Johannes Sprecher), his seeming opposite in manner and outlook; but at least a partial explanation may be found in Clodius's devotion to his own master, the learned but dissipated Mongiat, later immortalized, while Genoese ambassador to London, in the last portrait painted by the younger Holbein. One might add that it was Mongiat who as a young man set down the description, so precious to musicologists, of the singing of the Dublin-born Ahearne, when the latter joined the suite of Philip of Burgundy. Ahearne left writings of his own, but they have nothing to do with music, and they are in any event less interesting than the several extant letters of which he was the recipient: these include an account of the death of Romano the Gypsy, the first person to be burned as witch at Sprenger's instigation. The passage occurs in a letter from Alaric d'Abbeville, old but ever admired for the *Complainte de la Tronche* that he wrote when still a novice at the end of the Hundred Years War, whose legacy of desolation he so dolorously evokes. The poem, you will recall, is dedicated to Omo di Lucca, a Dantean scholar known to have spent nearly all his life in Florence, far from the haunts of Alaric — a fact that had bemused historians until recently, when it was discovered that Omo had accompanied Tommaso

Portinari to Bruges as tutor to his eldest daughter Benedetta. Lately I read that the studious couple, comprising a black-gowned doctor and a beautiful young girl, which illustrates a Book of Hours now in Beaune, depicts Omo and his charge. The miniature is the work of Michel de Douvre, an English artist not truly of Dover (very likely he arrived from Dover) but of York. He was reputedly a nephew of Nicholas Scriptor, a clerk renowned, towards the end of the preceding century, as the 'scribe's scribe'; he was the brother of Anne, abbess of the great Yorkshire convent of Poor Clares.

"Abbess Anne was a Stonebottle, the first known to us of the line that so brilliantly carried out the injunction of the family arms, *Floreat colus* ('Let the distaff flourish'). Her niece Judith Stonebottle, 'the English amazon,' fought conspicuously at Marignan in knight's disguise. Judith's second cousin Laetitia received the captaincy of a ship from Queen Elizabeth and explored Chesapeake Bay. Her descendant Emily Stonebottle constructed an observatory at York that was visited shortly before his death by an admiring Horrocks. Elizabeth Stonebottle, writing in York at the dawn of the Enlightenment, has been described as the 'well-oiled gate swinging between Locke and Voltaire.'

"The family's emigration to New York did not modify its lively tradition. The painter Catharine Stonebottle convinced Betsy Ross of the worthiness of stripes. Companion to Lewis and Clark, Patricia Stonebottle compiled exact geographical surveys of the West. Dr. Christina Stonebottle's work in battlefield surgery revolutionized practice during the First World War. Jane Horgus, née Stonebottle, erected the Elizabeth Palmer Peabody Bridge that is to be inaugurated this evening in the valley below us. Keep watching — the lights should go on any moment now."

Irritably, Robinson poked the lowering coals.

COUNTRY COOKING FROM CENTRAL FRANCE:
ROAST BONED ROLLED STUFFED SHOULDER OF LAMB *(FARCE DOUBLE)*

for Maxine Groffsky

Here is an old French regional dish for you to try. Attempts by presumptuous chefs to refine it have failed to subdue its basically hearty nature. It demands some patience, but you will be abundantly rewarded for your pains.

Farce double — literally, double stuffing — is the speciality of La Tour Lambert, a mountain village in Auvergne, that rugged heart of the Massif Central. I have often visited La Tour Lambert: the first time was in late May, when *farce double* is traditionally served. I have observed the dish being made and discussed it with local cooks.

The latter were skeptical about reproducing *farce double* elsewhere — not out of pride, but because they were afraid the dish would make no sense to a foreigner. (It is your duty to prove them wrong — and nothing would make them happier if you did.) Furthermore, they said, certain ingredients would be hard to find. Judicious substitution is our answer to that. Without it, after all, we would have to forgo most foreign cooking not out of a can.

The shoulder of lamb itself requires attention. You must buy it from a butcher who can dress it properly. Tell him to include the middle neck, the shoulder chops in the brisket, and part of the foreshank. The stuffing will otherwise fall out of the roast.

In Auvergne, preparing the cut is no problem, since whole lambs are roasted: the dish is considered appropriate for exceptional, often communal feasts, of a kind that has become a rarity with us.

All bones must be removed. If you leave this to the butcher, have him save them for the deglazing sauce. The fell or filament must be kept intact, or the flesh may crumble.

Set the boned forequarter on the kitchen table. Do not slice off the purple inspection stamps but scour them with a brush dipped in a weak solution of lye. The meat will need all the protection it can get. Rinse and dry.

Marinate the lamb in a mixture of 2 qts of white wine, 2 qts of olive oil, the juice of 16 lemons, salt, pepper, 16 crushed garlic cloves, 10 coarsely chopped yellow onions, basil, rosemary, melilot, ginger, allspice, and a handful of juniper berries. The juniper adds a pungent, authentic note. In Auvergne, shepherds pick the berries in late summer when they drive their flocks from the mountain pastures. They deposit the berries in La Tour Lambert, where they are pickled through the winter in cider brandy. The preparation is worth making, but demands foresight.

If no bowl is capacious enough for the lamb and its marinade, use a washtub. Without a tub, you must improvise. Friends of mine in Paris resort to their bidet; Americans may have to fall back on the kitchen sink, which is what I did the first time I made *farce double*. In La Tour Lambert, most houses have stone marinating troughs. Less favored citizens use the municipal troughs in the entrance of a cave in the hillside, just off the main square.

The lamb will have marinated satisfactorily in 5 or 6 days.

Allow yourself 3 hours for the stuffings. The fish balls or quenelles that are their main ingredient can be prepared a day in advance and refrigerated until an hour before use.

The quenelles of La Tour Lambert have traditionally been made from *chaste*, a fish peculiar to the mountain lakes of Auvergne. The name, a dialect word meaning "fresh blood," may have been suggested by the color of its spreading gills, through which it ingests its food. (It is a mouthless fish.) It is lured to the surface with a skein of tiny beads that resemble the larvae on which it preys, then bludgeoned with an underwater boomerang. *Chaste* has coarse, yellow-white flesh, with a mild but inescapable taste. It has been vaguely and mistakenly identified as a perch; our American perch, however, can replace it, provided it has been caught no more than 36 hours before cooking. Other substitutes are saltwater fish such as silver hake or green cod. If you use a dry-fleshed fish, remember to order beefkidney fat at the butcher's to add to the fish paste. (Be sure to grind it separately.)

To a saucepan filled with $2^1/_2$ cups of cold water, add salt, pepper, 2 pinches of grated nutmeg, and 6 tbsp of butter. Boil. Off heat, begin stirring in $2^1/_2$ cups of flour and continue as you again bring the water to a boil. Take off heat. Beat in 5 eggs, one at a time, then 5 egg whites. Let the liquid cool.

Earlier, you will have ground $3^3/_4$ lbs of fish with a mortar and pestle — heads, tails, bones, and all — and forced them through a coarse sieve. Do not use a grinder, blender, or cuisinart. The sieve of La Tour Lambert is an elegant sock of meshed copper wire, with a fitted ashwood plunger. It is kept immaculately bright. Its apertures are shrewdly gauged to mince the bones without pulverizing the fish. Into the strained fish, mix small amounts of salt, white pepper, nutmeg, and chopped truffles — fresh ones, if possible. (See TRUFFLE.)

Stir fish and liquid into an even paste.

Two hours before, you will have refrigerated 1 cup of the heaviest cream available. Here, of course, access to a cow is a blessing.

The breathtakingly viscid cream of La Tour Lambert is kept in specially excavated cellars. Those without one use the town chiller, in the middle depths — cool but not cold — of the cave mentioned earlier. Often I have watched the attendant women entering and emerging from that room, dusky figures in cowls, shawls, and long gray gowns, bearing earthenware jugs like offerings to a saint.

Beat the cool cream into the paste. Do it slowly: think of those erect, deliberate Auvergnat women as they stand in the faint gloom of the cave, beating with gestures of timeless calm. It should take at least 15 minutes to complete the task.

At some previous moment, you will have made the stuffing for the quenelles. (This is what makes the stuffing "double.") It consists of the milt of the fish and the sweetbreads of the lamb, both the neck and stomach varieties. (Don't forget to mention *them* to your butcher.) The milt is rapidly blanched. The sweetbreads are diced, salted, spiced with freshly ground hot pepper, and tossed for 6 minutes in clarified butter. Both are then chopped very fine (blender permitted) and kneaded into an unctuous mass with the help of 1 cup of lamb marrow and 3 tbsp of aged Madeira.

I said at the outset that I am in favor of appropriate substitutions in preparing *farce double:* but even though one eminent authority has suggested it, stuffing the quenelles with banana peanut butter is not appropriate.

The quenelles must now be shaped. Some writers who have discoursed at length on the traditional Auvergnat shape urge its adoption at all costs. I disagree. For the inhabitants of La Tour Lambert, who attach great significance to *farce double*, it may be right to feel strongly on this point. The same cannot be said for families in Maplewood or Orange County. You have enough to worry about as it is. If you are, however, an incurable stickler, you should know that in Auvergne molds are used. They are called *beurdes* (they are, coincidentally, shaped like birds), and they are available here. You can find them in any of the better head shops.

But forget about bird molds. Slap your fish paste onto a board and roll it flat. Spread on stuffing in parallel ½-inch bands 2 inches apart. Cut paste midway between bands, roll these strips into cylinders, and slice the cylinders into sections no larger than a small headache. Dip each piece in truffle crumbs. (See TRUFFLE.)

I refuse to become involved in the pros and cons of presteaming the quenelles. The only steam in La Tour Lambert is a rare fragrant wisp from the dampened fire of a roasting pit.

We now approach a crux in the preparation of *farce double:* enveloping the quenelles and binding them into the lamb. I must make a stern observation here; and you must listen to it. You must take it absolutely to heart.

If the traditional ways of enveloping the quenelles are arduous, they are in no way gratuitous. On them depends an essential component of *farce double,* namely the subtle interaction of lamb and fish. While the quenelles (and the poaching liquid that bathes them) must be largely insulated from the encompassing meat, they should not be wholly so. The quenelles must not be drenched in roasting juice or the lamb in fishy broth, but an exchange should occur, definite no matter how mild. Do not *under any circumstances* use a baggie or Saran Wrap to enfold the quenelles. Of course it's easier. So are TV dinners. For once, demand the utmost of yourself: the satisfaction will astound you, and *there is no other way.*

I mentioned this misuse of plastic to a native of La Tour Lambert. My interlocutor, as if appealing for divine aid, leaned back, lifted up his eyes, and stretched forth his arms. He was standing at the edge of a marinating trough; its edges were slick with marinade. One foot shot forward, he teetered for one moment on the brink, and then down he went. Dripping oil, encrusted with fragrant herbs, he emerged briskly and burst into tears.

There are two methods. I shall describe the first one briefly: it is the one used by official cooks for public banquets. Cawl (tripe skin) is scraped free of fat and rubbed with pumice stone to a thinness approaching nonexistence. This gossamer is sewn into an open pouch, which is filled with the quenelles and broth before being sewn shut. The sealing of the pouch is preposterously difficult. I have tried it six times; each time, ineluctable burstage has ensued. Even the nimble-fingered, thimble-thumbed seamstresses of La Tour Lambert find it hard. In their floodlit corner of the festal cave, they are surrounded by a sizable choir of wailing boys whose task is to aggravate their intention to a pitch of absolute sustained concentration. If the miracle always occurs, it is never less than miraculous.

The second method is to seal the quenelles inside a clay shell. This demands no supernatural skills, merely attention.

Purveyors of reliable cooking clay now exist in all major cities. The best are Italian. In New York, the most dependable are to be found in east Queens. (For addresses, see APPENDIX.)

Stretch and tack down two 18-inch cheesecloth squares. Sprinkle until soaking (mop up puddles, however). Distribute clay in pots and roll flat until entire surface is evenly covered. The layer of clay should be no more than $1/16$-inch thick. Scissor edges clean.

Drape each square on an overturned 2-qt bowl. Fold back flaps. Mold into hemispheres. Check fit, then dent edge of each hemisphere with forefinger so that when dents are facing each other, they form a $3/4$-inch hole.

Be sure to prepare the shell at least 48 hours in advance so that it hardens properly. (If you are a potter, you can bake it in the oven; if not, you risk cracking.) As the drying clay flattens against the cheese-cloth, tiny holes will appear. Do *not* plug them. Little will pass through them: just enough to allow the necessary exchange of savors.

Make the poaching liquid — 3 qts of it — like ordinary fish stock (q.v.). The wine used for this in Auvergne is of a local sparkling vari-ety not on the market; but any good champagne is an acceptable substitute.

By "acceptable substitute," I mean one acceptable to me. Purists have cited the fish stock as a reason for not making *farce double* at all. In La Tour Lambert, they rightly assert, the way the stock is kept allows it to evolve without spoiling: in the amphoralike jars that are stored in the coldest depths of the great cave, a faint, perpetual fer-mentation gives the perennial brew an exquisite, violet-flavored sour-ness. This, they say, is inimitable. I say that 30 drops of decoction of elecampane blossoms will reproduce it so perfectly as to convince the most vigilant tongue.

Fifteen minutes before roasting time, put the quenelles in one of the clay hemispheres. Set the other against it, dent to dent. Seal the seam with clay, except for the hole, and thumb down well. Hold the sphere in one hand with the hole on top. With a funnel, pour in hot poaching liquid until it overflows, then empty 1 cup of liquid. This is to keep the shell from bursting from within when the broth reaches a boil.

Be sure to keep the shell in your hand: set in a bowl, one bash against its side will postpone your dinner for several days at least. In La Tour Lambert, where even more fragile gut is used, the risks are lessened by placing the diaphanous bags in woolen reticules. It is still incredible that no damage is ever done to them on the way to the stuffing tables. To avoid their cooling, they are carried at a run by teenage boys, for whom this is a signal honor: every Sunday throughout the following year, they will be allowed to wear their unmistakable lily-white smocks.

Earlier in the day, you will have anointed the lamb, inside and out: inside, with fresh basil, coriander leaves, garlic, and ginger thickly crushed into walnut oil (this is a must); outside, with mustard powder mixed with — ideally — wild boar fat. I know that wild boars do not roam our woods (sometimes, on my walks through Central Park, I feel I may soon meet one): bacon fat will do — about a pint of it.

You will have left the lamb lying outside down. Now nestle the clay shell inside the boneless cavity. Work it patiently into the fleshy nooks, then urge the meat in little bulges around it, pressing the lamb next to the shell, not against it, with the gentlest possible nudges. When the shell is deeply ensconced, fold the outlying flaps over it, and shape the whole into a regular square cushion roast. Sew the edges of the meat together, making the seams hermetically tight.

If the original roasting conditions will surely exceed your grasp, a description of them may clarify your goals.

In Auvergne, the body of the lamb is lowered on wetted ropes into a roasting pit. It comes to rest on transverse bars set close to the floor of the pit. Hours before, ash boughs that have dried through three winters are heaped in the pit and set ablaze: by now they are embers. These are raked against the four sides and piled behind wrought-iron grids into glowing walls. The cast-iron floor stays hot from the fire. When the lamb is in place, a heated iron lid is set over the pit. The lid does more than refract the heat from below. Pierced with a multitude of small holes, it allows for aspersions of water on coals that need damping and the sprinkling of oil on the lamb, which is thus basted throughout its roasting in a continuous fine spray. Previously, I might add, the lamb has been rapidly seared over an open fire. Four senior cooks manage this by standing on high stepladders and manipulating the poles and extensible thongs used to shift the animal, which they precisely revolve over the flames so that it receives an even grilling.

Thus the onslaught of heat to which the lamb is subjected is, while too restrained to burn it, intense enough to raise the innermost broth to the simmering point.

Carefully lower the lamb into a 25-inch casserole. (If you have no such casserole, buy one. If it will not fit in your oven, consider this merely one more symptom of the shoddiness of our age, which the popularity of dishes like *farce double* may someday remedy.) Cover. You will have turned on the oven at maximum heat for 45 minutes at least. Close the oven door and lower the thermostat to 445°. For the next 5 hours, there is nothing to do except check the oven thermometer occasionally and baste the roast with juices from the casserole every 10 minutes. If you feel like catnapping, have no compunctions about it. Do not have anything to drink — considering what lies in store for you, it is a foolish risk. The genial cooks of La Tour Lambert may fall to drinking, dancing, and singing at this point, but remember that they have years of experience behind them; and you, unlike them, must act alone.

One song always sung during the roasting break provides valuable insight into the character of the Auvergnat community. It tells the story of a blacksmith's son who sets out to find his long-lost mother. She is dead, but he cannot remember her death, nor can he accept it. His widowed father has taken as second wife a pretty woman younger than himself. She is hardly motherly towards her stepson: one day, after he has grown to early manhood, she seduces him — in the words of the song, "she does for him what mother never did for her son." This line recurs throughout as a refrain.

It is after the shock of this event that the son leaves in quest of his mother. His father repeatedly tries to dissuade him, insisting that she is dead, or that, if she is alive, it is only in a place "as near as the valley beyond the hill and far away as the stars." In the end, however, he gives his son a sword and a purse full of money and lets him go. The stepmother, also hoping to keep the son from leaving, makes another but this time futile attempt to "do for him what mother never did for her son."

At the end of three days, the son comes to a city. At evening he meets a beautiful woman with long red hair. She offers him hospitality, which he accepts, and she attends lovingly to his every want. Pleasure and hope fill his breast. He begins wondering. He asks himself if this woman might not be his lost mother. But when night falls, the red-haired woman takes him into her bed and "does for him what mother never did for her son." The son knows she cannot be the one he seeks. Pretending to sleep, he waits for an opportunity to leave her; but, at midnight, he sees her draw a length of strong, sharp cord from beneath her pillow and stretch it towards him. The son leaps up, seizes his sword, and confronts the woman. Under its threat, she confesses that she was planning to murder him for the sake of his purse, as she has done with countless travelers: their corpses lie rotting in her cellar. The son slays the woman with his sword, wakes up a nearby priest to assure a Christian burial for her and her victims, and goes his way.

Three days later, he arrives at another city. As day wanes, a strange woman again offers him hospitality, and again he accepts. She is even more beautiful than the first; and her hair is also long, but golden. She lavishes her attentions on the young man, and in such profusion that hope once again spurs him to wonder whether she might not be his lost mother. But with the coming of darkness, the woman with the golden hair takes him into her bed and "does for him what mother never did for her son." His hopes have again been disappointed. Full of unease, he feigns sleep. Halfway through the night he hears footsteps mounting the stairs. He scarcely has time to leap out of bed and grasp his sword before two burly villains come rushing into the room. They attack him, and he cuts them down. Then, turning on the woman, he forces her at swordpoint to confess that she had hoped to make him her prisoner and sell him into slavery. Saracen pirates would have paid a high price for one of such strength and beauty. The son slays her, wakes up a priest to see that she and her henchmen receive Christian burial, and goes his way.

Another three days' journey brings him to a third city. There, at end of day, the son meets still another fair woman, the most beautiful of all, with flowing, raven-black hair. Alone of the three, she seems to recognize him; and when she takes him under her roof and bestows on him more comfort and affection than he had ever dreamed possible, he knows that this time his hope cannot be mistaken. But when night comes, she takes him into her bed, and she, like the others, "does for him what mother never did for her son." She has drugged his food. He cannot help falling asleep; only, at midnight, the touch of cold iron against his throat rouses him from his stupor. Taking up his sword, he points it in fury at the breast of the woman who has so beguiled him. She begs him to leave her in peace, but she finally acknowledges that she meant to cut his throat and suck his blood. She is an old, old witch who has lost all her powers but one, that of preserving her youth. This she does by drinking the blood of young men. The son runs her through with his sword. With a weak cry, she falls to the floor a wrinkled crone. The son knows that a witch cannot be buried in consecrated ground, and he goes his way.

But the young man travels no further. He is bitterly convinced of the folly of his quest; he has lost all hope of ever finding his mother; wearily he turns homeward.

On his way he passes through the cities where he had first faced danger. He is greeted as a hero. Thanks to the two priests, all know that it was he who destroyed the evil incarnate in their midst. But he takes no pride in having killed two women who "did for him what mother never did for her son."

On the ninth day of his return, he sees, from the mountain pass he has reached, the hill beyond which his native village lies. In the valley between, a shepherdess is watching her flock. At his approach she greets him tenderly, for she knows the blacksmith's son and has loved him for many years. He stops with her to rest. She has become, he notices, a beautiful young woman — not as beautiful, perhaps, as the evil three: but her eyes are wide and deep, and her long hair is brown.

The afternoon goes by. Still the son does not leave. At evening, he partakes of the shepherdess's frugal supper. At nighttime, when she lies down, he lies down beside her; and she, her heart brimming with gladness, "does for him what mother never did for her son." The shepherdess falls asleep. The son cannot sleep; and he is appalled, in the middle of the night, to see the shepherdess suddenly rise up beside him. But she only touches his shoulder as if to waken him and points to the starry sky. She tells him to look up. There, she says, beyond the darkness, the souls of the dead have gathered into one blazing light. With a cry of pain, the son asks, "Then is my mother there?" The shepherdess answers that she is. His mother lives beyond the stars, and the stars themselves are chinks in the night through which the fateful light of the dead and the unborn is revealed to the world. "Oh, Mother, Mother," the young man weeps. The shepherdess then says to him, "Who is now mother to your sleep and waking? Who else can be the mother of your joy and pain? I shall henceforth be the mother of every memory; and from this night on, I alone am your mother — even if now, and tomorrow, and all the days of my life, I do for you what mother never did for her son." In his sudden ecstasy, the blacksmith's son understands. He has discovered his desire.

And so, next morning, he brings the shepherdess home. His father, when he sees them, weeps tears of relief and joy; and his stepmother, sick with remorse, welcomes them as saviors. Henceforth they all live in mutual contentment; and when, every evening, the approach of darkness kindles new yearning in the young man's heart and he turns to embrace his wife, she devotedly responds and never once fails, through the long passing years, to "do for him what mother never did for her son."

The connection of this song with *farce double* lies, I was told, in an analogy between the stars and the holes in the lid of the roasting pit.

When your timer sounds for the final round, you must be in fighting trim: not aggressive, but supremely alert. You now have to work at high speed and with utmost delicacy. The meat will have swelled in cooking: it is pressing against the clay shell harder than ever, and one jolt can spell disaster. Do not coddle yourself by thinking that this pressure is buttressing the shell. In La Tour Lambert, the handling of the cooked lamb is entrusted to squads of highly trained young men: they are solemn as pallbearers and dexterous as shortstops, and their virtuosity is eloquent proof that this is no time for optimism.

Slide the casserole slowly out of the oven and gently set it down on a table covered with a thrice-folded blanket. You will now need help. Summon anyone — a friend, a neighbor, a husband, a lover, a sibling, even a guest — so that the two of you can slip four broad wooden spatulas under the roast, one on each side, and ease it onto a platter. The platter should be resting on a soft surface such as a cushion or a mattress (a small hammock would be perfect). Wait for the meat to cool before moving it onto anything harder. Your assistant may withdraw.

Meanwhile attend to the gravy. No later than the previous evening, you will have made $1^1/_2$ qts of stock with the bones from the lamb shoulder, together with the customary onions, carrots, celery, herb bouquet, cloves, scallions, parsnips, and garlic (see STOCK), to which you must not hesitate to add any old fowl, capon, partridge, or squab carcasses that are gathering rime in your deep freeze, or a young rabbit or two. Pour out the fat in the casserole and set it on the stove over high heat. Splash in enough of the same good champagne to scrape the casserole, clean, and boil. When the wine has largely evaporated, take off heat, and add 2 cups of rendered pork fat. Set the casserole over very low heat and make a quick *roux* or brown sauce with 3 cups of flour. Then slowly pour in 2 cups of the blood of the lamb, stirring it in a spoonful at a time. Finally, add the stock. Raise the heat to medium high and let the liquid simmer down to the equivalent of 13 cupfuls.

While the gravy reduces, carefully set the platter with the roast on a table, resting one side on an object the size of this cookbook, so that it sits at a tilt. Place a broad shallow bowl against the lower side. If the clay shell now breaks, the poaching broth will flow rapidly into the bowl. Prop the lamb with a wooden spoon or two to keep it from sliding off the platter. Slit the seams in the meat, spread its folds, and expose the clay shell. Put on kitchen gloves — the clay will be scalding — and coax the shell from its depths. Set it in a saucepan, give it a smart crack with a mallet, and remove the grosser shards. Ladle out the quenelles and keep them warm in the oven in a covered, buttered dish with a few spoonfuls of broth. Strain the rest of the liquid, reduce it quickly to a quarter of its volume, and then use what is left of the champagne to make a white sauce as explained on p. 888. Nap the quenelles with sauce and serve.

If you have worked fast and well, by the time your guests finish the quenelles, the lamb will have set long enough for its juices to have withdrawn into the tissues without its getting cold. Pour the gravy into individual heated bowls. Place a bowl in front of each guest, and set the platter with the lamb, which you will have turned outside up, at the center of the table. The meat is eaten without knives and forks. Break off a morsel with the fingers of the right hand, dip it in gravy, and pop it into your mouth. In Auvergne, this is managed with nary a dribble; but lobster bibs are a comfort.

(Do not be upset if you yourself have lost all desire to eat. This is a normal, salutary condition. Your satisfaction will have been in the doing, not in the thing done. But observe the reaction of your guests, have a glass of wine [see below], and you may feel the urge to try one bite, and perhaps a second . . .)

It is a solemn moment when, at the great communal spring banquet, the Mayor of La Tour Lambert goes from table to table and with shining fingers gravely breaks the skin of each lamb. After this ceremony, however, the prevailing gaiety reasserts itself. After all, the feast of *farce double* is not only a time-hallowed occasion but a very pleasant one. It is a moment for friendships to be renewed, for enemies to forgive one another, for lovers to embrace. At its origin, curiously enough, the feast was associated with second marriages (some writers think this gave the dish its name). Such marriages have never been historically explained; possibly they never took place. What is certain is that the feast has always coincided with the arrival, from the lowlands, of shepherds driving their flocks to the high pastures where they will summer. Their coming heralds true spring and its first warmth; and it restores warmth, too, between the settled mountain craftsmen of La Tour Lambert and the semi-nomadic shepherds from the south. The two communities are separate only in their ways of life. They have long been allied by esteem, common interest, and, most important, by blood. Marriages between them have been recorded since the founding of the village in the year one thousand; and if many a shepherd's daughter has settled in La Tour Lambert as the wife of a wheelwright or turner, many an Auvergnat son, come autumn, has left his father's mill or forge to follow the migrant flocks towards Les Saintes-Maries-de-la-Mer. Perhaps the legend of second marriages reflects a practice whereby a widow or a widower took a spouse among the folk of which he was not a member. The eating of *farce double* would then be exquisitely appropriate; for there is no doubt at all that the composition of the dish — lamb from the plains by the sea, fish from lakes among the grazing lands — deliberately embodies the merging of these distinct peoples in one community. I should add that at the time the feast originated, still another group participated harmoniously in its celebration: pilgrims from Burgundy on their way to Santiago de Compostela. Just as the people of La Tour Lambert provided fish for the great banquet and the shepherds contributed their lambs, the pilgrims supplied kegs of new white wine that they brought with them from Chassagne, the Burgundian village now called Chassagne-Montrachet. Their wine became the invariable accompaniment for both parts of *farce double;* and you could hardly do better than to adopt the custom. Here, at least, tradition can be observed with perfect fidelity.

It is saddening to report that, like the rest of the world, La Tour Lambert has undergone considerable change. Shepherds no longer walk their flocks from the south but ship them by truck. The lakes have been fished out, and a substitute for *chaste* is imported frozen from Yugoslavia. The grandson of the last wheelwright works in the tourist bureau, greeting latterday pilgrims who bring no wine. He is one of the very few of his generation to have remained in the village. (The cement quarry, which was opened with great fanfare ten years ago as a way of providing jobs, employs mainly foreign labor. Its most visible effect has been to shroud the landscape in white dust.) I have heard, however, that the blacksmith still earns a good living making wrought-iron lamps. Fortunately, the future of *farce double* is assured, at least for the time being. The festal cave has been put on a commercial footing, and it now produces the dish for restaurants in the area all year round (in the off-season, on weekends only). It is open to the public. I recommend a visit if you pass nearby.

Eat the quenelles ungarnished. Mashed sorrel goes nicely with the lamb.

Serves thirteen.

THE NETWORK

Howemver, please. Please.

It's no use, anyway.

In a daze, however, as good as death or a bad cold, crossed the avenue from that café. Had forgotten moreover to piss. Resorted to a hotel lobby, however: "Second on left." This was wrong: a flight of metal steps led down into powdery dusk, in an atmosphere of steamship depths, through which gazed anyway from a warm railing. Not for long, however:

The sensation of upheaval was not missing and not ignored through the pain, accompanied by the struggle moreover for a defining concept, such as "derrick hook in back." However, breath was stunned out of the lungs into a shrunk ball stuffed between brain and cranium. There was the jolt, the jolting effect anyway, that also contained the pain. The point of impact, however, lay between the shoulder blades, but numbness instantly gripped the whole spine, quickly enough to precede the inability to shout. Arms and legs thrust straight out to dangle quivering, with fecal drift; there was no time for dangling, moreover — the swathing had commenced. Already there was, however, no more notion of time spans. It was done with a supple tape, not describable as wet (this point is doubtful anyway because of the novocaine drench). Included were irritating kinks of clothing, however; there was of course no room for chafing, because the twine was tight and there was so much of it, three layers applied, to the sound of its hissed expulsion, in diagonal ball-of-string fashion: but the unpleasant thought struck of having crumpled twine bunched behind a knee forever. The turds were less worrisome, drying moreover through all that spaghetti. Of smells, sperm was the last, however, and saddest.

Transferal took place in three stages, with wall flake, pipe bundles, and lone bulbs passing in a detached flatness, perhaps from the loss of depth perception or of one eye: first, laterally to a position among swaying cables; second, upwards, to be glued to a joist; third, far down, finally moored anyway to the cloth hide of a pipe, with hot hushed rushing.

Dreaming followed, however, as in dozy reading, e.g.: measles nap — green gloom; peering from the sheet cavern; hunting cool pillow areas. The pipe was, moreover, hot — will it scorch? However can't care but not in its interest.

The spine pain anyway is fixed throughout the length of the body forever, it has been decided. What about sleep, however?

And, e.g., a summer swim, climbing onto a bank to dry, stickily moreover. Two flies abandoned, however, the warm turf. Anyway it was then I encountered the long structures. A mild breeze, however, had risen. They were bright, pliant poles, some bending some still, in sleek sheaths moreover. However, were they alive, or a coralline marvel? They were bearably hot. Anyway, floating among them in a medium like water, and like air, I came to rest on a hummock of sponge strands fitted in an interstice, mossy, snuggish even in their moister layers. The pink stems inclined above me; I nestled in the plumy feelers and, striking into gumminess, subsided against this dull apprehension.

REMARKS OF THE SCHOLAR GRADUATE

The headmaster has asked me to give you boys, briefly and in plain language, a resumé of my work. I know that as with all scientific discoveries mine has been doubly misrepresented to the lay world — by half-comprehending news media on one hand, by professional journals with their confusing jargon on the other. Then there have been the dust clouds of controversy shrouding further what is essentially not a difficult set of facts. And I'm glad of this occasion not only because of the pleasure of paying modest homage to the school where I acquired the first tools of scholarship, but because as regards the controversy I want to repeat — well, that is not quite honest, let me rather say assert, something that could not be admitted earlier lest my whole hypothesis be disgraced: Gartner was right. At least he was, as far as his main claim was concerned, not wrong. I am sorry the old man is dead, dead before I could give him due credit.

Indeed we must start with Gartner's theory, which I now consider proved: that the horizontal line, or dash, was a non-phonetic symbol of the ancient Bactrian divinity, derived from its incarnation as a snake. The discovery last month of some tablets from about 2500 B.C. furnish the proof. On them the sign appears sometimes singly, often by twos, threes, and fives, almost always in arrangements of less than seven. Previously we had always considered such small groups as fragments, or fakes. While it is true that on these tablets many of the dashlike strokes vary considerably from strict horizontality, this is nothing new, and in any case the deformations have no significance — since there was but one sign, its shape could deviate from the norm without danger of ambiguity. Is there any chalk available? Good, let me show you —

and so forth: all one and the same thing.

So here we have without any doubt a people whose scriptural apparatus comprised one symbol, a stylized pictogram of their god, arbitrary, particular, charged with connotations that we cannot hope to disclose. This was Gartner's discovery and it is a fine one. But it ends where it begins, and its usefulness is limited to the very first, most primitive period of Bactrian written culture. For Gartner refused to explore any possible extension, evolution, or modification of the initial significance that he had rightfully attributed to the symbol. He would not even admit that the dash might have come to stand — and what could be more logical? — for the *name* of the god as well as for the god himself; this would have meant acknowledging that the dash had gained a rudimentary phonetic power. Such obstinacy led to the complete breakdown of his reasoning powers when he came to consider the Early Second Period of Bactrian civilization (about 2000 to 1850 B.C.).

Except for one or two fragmentary examples, all the materials of the Early Second Period (tablets, seals, etcetera) show the dash assembled into vertical groups of seven, so:

————————
————————
————————
————————
————————
————————
————————

Gartner, and all other scholars until myself have followed him, saw in these columns only a multiplication of the original symbol, and they consequently interpreted them as mere reduplications or intensifications of its prime significance. In other words they saw in them only a quantitative transformation of identity. But the fact is, the dashes are *not* identical.

Again I must eliminate any thought of giving importance to physical variations of the sign. It is incredible how scholars persist in dashing down this well-pounded dead-end street, even though our oldest testimony on the original Bactrians, a paragraph in Herodotus, excludes all doubt on the subject: "The few remaining Old Bactrians say that until the time of the calamity they wrote with a single letter. Some attribute their demise to the abandonment of the original practice." No, when I say that the dashes when grouped by sevens are not alike, I mean simply this. The dash at the bottom is, uniquely, the dash at the bottom. The one above it is not at the bottom, and by that virtue is unlike the first. The one above that is similarly distinct from the two below it. So it goes through the topmost one.

If I can claim to have had an original idea, this is it. It is certainly not one that presupposes arcane knowledge of any sort, or a departure from common modes of thought. But because it was new and because the rest of my hypothesis flowed naturally from it, it was denounced as fantastic by most of my colleagues, and it brought me years of dispute and abuse. I cannot go into all that argument here. Ultimately the confrontations were useful, led me to new truths, and helped me refine those already discovered. I can only summarize the facts that issued from that long and difficult time, omitting the sometimes lucky, sometimes devious ways by which I came to them.

We have therefore a group of seven symbols identical in form but distinguished from one another by position. It was highly probable, once one had posited a phonetic significance to this differentiation (pictogrammatic and thus conceptional distinctions were excluded by the visual equivalence of the signs), that the ancient Bactrians like their neighbors indicated only the consonants of the words they transcribed; and while it was impossible to be sure exactly which consonants were represented by the dashes, extrapolation from later texts was able to establish the classes of consonants that could be assigned them, thus:

$$\text{_____k} \quad \text{(h)}$$
$$\text{_____l} \quad \text{(r)}$$
$$\text{_____sh} \quad \text{(ch, j)}$$
$$\text{_____t} \quad \text{(d, n)}$$
$$\text{_____s} \quad \text{(z)}$$
$$\text{_____f} \quad \text{(v)}$$
$$\text{_____p} \quad \text{(b, m)}$$

(For convenience I shall henceforth let the first letter stand for its class.) Next I discovered that vowels were also determined by position, that is, they were represented by the spaces between the dashes:

(a)

---
a
---
e
---
i
---
u
---
o
---
a

(a)

Finally, I learned that the symbols were to be read from the bottom up:

(a)
k
a
l
e
sh
i
t   =*(a)pafosutishelak(a)*
u
s
o
f
a
p
(a)

This was — schematically, approximately — the written word. It was of course *the* written word — no other could be set down, as a moment's reflection will show: there were seven characters to be sure, but only as a function of their place in a fixed sequence. Every word (so to speak) had to begin with *pa*, continue with *fo*, and so forth — hence only one word was possible. The unique case that defined the symbols was all they themselves could signify. Because of this singularity, I myself have no doubt that the seven dashes stood for the seven syllables of the Bactrian divinity. The first and only word was the first and only name, which was affixed to all things, so that all things bore the name of God.

The first step in phonetic differentiation, which was albeit limited of crucial importance, was followed around 1850 B.C. (Middle Second Period) by a new development in Bactrian writing. Whereas until then only single groups of dashes are found, now several columns appear on the tablets and (another novelty) stones:

etc.

What can this signify? Isn't the answer obvious? We need only apply our experience of the Bactrian mentality to guess that as the position of the dashes in a column determined their function, so the positions of the columns in a line determines theirs. It is a pity that this period of Bactrian writing is so shortlived and that we cannot with certainty say which of two possible forms this linear determination of meaning took: whether the words were all the same while their denotation silently varied; or whether the words themselves changed with their denotations. Although the latter alternative will seem more reasonable to us, there is no particular evidence to make us prefer it. For instance, the Fobsuk Stele reads:

and we know from a Sanskrit version on the back that the sense is "God copulates with the soul of mother," but it is by no means sure that, as my colleague Piotrovsky states, the corresponding words are

mavozunijerah	(of) mother
apafozunijlaka	heart
amavosudishlah	dig a well (in)
pafosutishelaka	god

although of course this would be quite possible in the later texts from which he derives his interpretation. They may simply be:

(a)pafosutishelak(a)
     (a)pafosutishelak(a)
          (a)pafosutishelak(a)
               (a)pafosutishelak(a)

where the first (that is, rightmost) (a)pafosutishelak(a) would mean "god," the second "copulate with," the third "soul," and the last "mother."

The question is not an essential one. The fact is that the first group in a line has a given meaning, the second another one, and so on.

There was no theoretical limit to the number of columns that could be aligned, nor was the line itself a practical limit: the Bactrians soon learned to set rows of columns one above another to form a continuity. The longest text contains eighty-seven groups, in seven and a half rows. The majority of examples, however, range from four to seven columns. There are none with less than four. This is because the statements, whatever their length, were obliged to begin with the words "God copulates with the soul of (the) mother," this was in fact the cardinal sense of all declarations in the new writing, so that all its written utterances were inevitably religious in nature or at least given a strongly religious coloring by these opening words. In fact we may say that where in the first period Bactrian writing consisted of one divine name that was identified with all things, in the second period it consisted of a statement of one divine act that was identified with all acts. The change corresponds to that in religious belief from a magical to a moral god, to that in economy from agriculture to trade.

You will have noticed that in Piotrovsky's version of the Fobsuk

Stele, the *e* has in two of the four words fallen from the normal series of vowels. This is in accordance with the subsequent evolution of the Bactrian tongue and script. The unlimited possibilities of aligning groups, which differed radically from the earlier closed field of seven characters, evidently took the lid off the scribes' inventiveness. In a matter of two generations, by 1800 B.C., the system of uniform columns has broken down (Late Second Period). Groups were divided into fractions that represented an increasingly various number of phonetic objects, including vowels, dipthongs, and syllables:

These fractions lost more and more of their relation to the original sounds of the groups, and of course to the sacred meanings of the original words, or word. As the complexity of the script grew, vertical or diagonal marks were appended to the dashes to specify their functions, although the seven levels of the dashes were retained until a surprisingly late date. Thus a row of characters had the height of a row of columns:

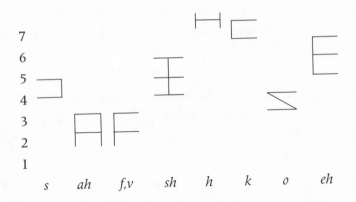

This last reminder of its origins disappeared from the alphabet (for such it now was) just before the destruction of the Bactrian state and the dispersion of its people. The history of their preservation of the script and its reemergence in Europe is the subject of my next book — and touching as your attentive faces are, I don't plan to give away any of its secrets today. But perhaps I may point out to you that ten Bactrian characters survive in the modern international alphabet of our own time; that they occupy the first six positions in it, as well as — and this is the most telling of all — the first and the last. This is history's certain homage to the unapproachable superiority of the Bactrians among the ancients in the domain of writing.

Of course Gartner would have none of this. He railed on to the end of his life, poor man, against everything I wrote. He was obsessed with the *shapes* of the sign! He even called me a "chauvinistic liar"! The words are preposterous, but after all not surprising, coming as they did — and this is something you boys should remember — from a man of the West.

THE LEDGE

The dawn fog separated into two parts. The lower, a bluish translucent white, sank to earth in the shape of a lens, its edges resting against the bases of the mountains that defined the valley, its mass curving over the vague residue of the city. The upper part rose steadily, in silvery layers, like jellyfish gliding toward the surface of the ocean, in ever-increasing transparency. Into a cleft in the side of the valley a portion of the thinning fog was diverted from its ascent, was sucked into a bunched white river of cloud that flowed south, rising along the bed of the gorge that indented the mountain, to issue several miles farther on a high plateau. The cloud-river there flattened out over fields, enclosing the infrequent hamlets in moments of apparent bad weather, through which however the sun quickly penetrated, as the moisture continued its lateral dispersion. The valley-born cloud was no longer a cloud, but an airy emulsion that tended toward the spruce forests on the hills edging the plateau, where it hung amid the dark trees long after the open areas had cleared. But other, truer clouds now appeared among and above the hills. For instance, to the south, puffs like explosions sailed into view; it is true that they did not last long. To the east where the higher hills lay, loglike clouds surged as the day warmed — they resembled the gorge cloud but were of a robuster nature, they did not cling in the forests but pushed over them, and even the hills did not alter the direction, only the inclination, of their advance. In the west, far away, flattish yellow-gray clouds drifted, looking as if they had lain between the pages of undusted tomes. Stared at, they were never seen to alter their position or shape. Yet after a glance to the north, where a tournament was about to start between contestants using cloud blocks, the western clouds had become unrecognizable: although still flat and immobile, they were in new parts of that section of the sky, and their outlines were no longer like chips but like blades. It was to those northern apparitions, however, that attention was directed during the noon and afternoon hours, not only because of the attractiveness of moving curves deployed on a grand scale, but because the spectacle was at once satisfyingly dramatic and satisfyingly remote. In fact those toppling towers seemed attached to the rim of a circle at whose center we, on the edge of the plateau, remained indefatigably vigilant: thus they rolled, flattening as they sank, slowly around from north to west and, at dusk, a little beyond. During their revolution they changed in color from cold-gray-tinged white through strawy yellow, in which the gray took on a darker tone, faint gold, rust, and red to black, black at first streaked with sunset hues, then thick black. By this time the westerly flat clouds had risen high enough to refract daylight a while longer; and to the east the several logs of cloud had fused in one vast layer — it slides over the hilltops toward us like smoke from dry ice. The sky to the south is empty, and accompanied by the redness of the lofty western clouds, fluffed out now, this might lead us to expect a clear morning, but that anticipation is soon belied by the night sky, a sky of stars few and blurred.

THEIR WORDS, FOR YOU

Another morning, another egg. The sky was up early. It had rained all night: to you and me sleeping, the storm was a delight. In the east, morning clouds are building a kingdom of red and silver. Time for you to get up! Come into the kingdom of morning delight and come as king! Come into the omelet of morning delight, and come as egg!

You can't make an omelet without breaking half a dozen of the other. Take six eggs . . . Eggs are things — eggs were things: have an omelet. Have a little bread with it too. Cat! Come on Cat, you old dog, have a little bread till it's bone time.

You're looking good today. What of going down the road to the port? No — you propose old-stone-gathering at the waterside, and going into the water when the tide comes in.

You go with me down fences that teach the intentions of the men that dispose of the grass. A horse waits at a fence; another rolls on the grass, breaking wind. (Good for the horse — one should break wind when one has to, putting it off does no good.) At the side of the road dead grass is burning, old sticks and grass, burning silver in the morning. The road is a delight, with water on one side, oaks and grass on the other; and the grass leads away to another water. In the oaks you once gathered bird's eggs from moss.

From the road you can see the port, the old port paved with stones, paved with bones. Sailors gather in it at night, gathering on the night side of the port looking for the tricks and stitches of love.

> *God disposes*
> > *Red sky at night,*
> *Man proposes*
> > *Sailor's delight*

When the tide is coming in, sailors can drink and sleep. In the morning all leave on the early tide. Not all: a few go on sleeping.

II

Men that had been sailors came to be men of roads and grass. A dozen men proposed to build the roads. Others disposed the fences. Men broke stones to pave and build. The men break new bread and drink new water, and pour new water over their hands.

Not all took to the new kingdom (one with no king). Water can look good even to a one-eyed sailor — "a sailor with no love of water is an unlucky man" — and sailors that had the love went off on new tides. Soon a port was built — built, it has been taught, with the bones of dead men, dead sailors. Soon the stones of the port looked green with moss, and silver with gatherings of birds.

Other sailors took to building, and making things, and being men of oaks and grass, and horse men. "A sailor on a horse had better be lucky" — but half a dozen times teaches even unlucky men when their intentions are mighty. From east to west the grasses were gathered, and stone and oak were built up to the sky — no, not to the sky: but a new kingdom was made.

You go with me into a break in the fence, on which suckers are growing. On the other side a man is teaching a horse, "breaking" him. The horse — red, shy, and mighty — is looking into the wind. The man is looking away from the wind — he is looking at the horse. He leads him with one hand, having a stick in the other.

You led me to the water. The tide was down, leaving many stones to look at, green and red, with tide water lying in the lining of the stones. Birds that had waited when the tide was in have gathered at the water's side, downwind.

You go into the water. But it's no time for stone gathering. From the water to the west a new wind is blowing, and to the west a storm is building, coming with the wind. All at once it's time to go away. In a storm it is the fool that takes to the water.

Getting to the road you called to me, "It's going to rain cats and dogs!" And soon the wind pours down the waters it has gathered.

In the oaks by the side of the road, old men had been playing cards on the grass. When the storm broke, other men left off building and came to play with the old men, waiting till the storm blew on. One old man lay sleeping. You waited with me a little away from the men playing and sleeping: "Mighty oaks in a storm."

It was raining on every side. The storm paved the sky with stone.

Let it rain; let the wind blow. Down kingdoms of grass and stone the wind teaches you: wait. Wait, and sleep. The wind will blow, the night will come, the storm will break. We shall go into the night to sleep, the night in which, as in words, mouths meet.

III

In the night, water poured from the sky, to call up in the morning a new tide of worms — which with the water will make for better grass. The rain went away early, as the east went from silver to silver-and-red. The night was done, and what a night! Not water and a dozen devils could have spoiled it. A night of love: in which you made me come twice, and once in the morning. Don't let the words make you red and shy!

The break of day proposes new things: new bread, for one. Bread makes the morning. Look! in the east, red bread loaf clouds. But the little clouds the wind rolls down the grass look green. The fences look green too: the storm has made old fences new.

Six birds break from a green cloud and go off. Other little birds gather for the bread you'll give. A redbird! Shy birds gather on the even grass, going up and down before coming up to the water to drink and play. Others wait on a fence. And in the bushes wait the cats. As it is, cats can wait for six tomorrows, it won't harm the birds and it won't do the cats any good. As soon as a bird takes in a cat's intention, it leaves the grass and takes to a bush; in time leaves the bush to take to an oak; and soon a cat is looking down from the green oak . . .

From early morning every bird has been calling to every other bird, making their intentions mighty: "*My* worms, *my* worms . . ."

On the other side of the fence, two little dogs are rolling on the grass. Have they been taught to come when called? Look — the dogs are coming without a word from you. Good dogs, that come at once. (But *better* dogs do not come without being called.)

No, it isn't for you. The dogs are coming over to look at another man. The one coming down the other side of the fence, the one you've met before. Can't *you* put him off? Don't let the loaf burn.

Soon two other dogs meet the first two. It's the cook's dogs — lucky dogs to be a cook's! One is waiting to play "get the stick." Good. With a stick one can teach a dog many tricks, when one does it with love.

But when the other dogs came, the cats left, all six. Even one dog can dispose of many a cat; and when dogs gather, cats take the intention to be other than that of burying bones. When one chooses a dog, it is better for the good of one's little kingdom to get a dog that can lie down with a cat and play with it.

You go off to propose things to the other man. Always playing the fool — you, not him: playing the fool is a delight fools cannot have. But every man has a side worth looking at — once.

Another, one-eyed dog has come and is making water on the side of the oak.

Waiting for him to go away. The wind has broken up the sky of clouds, it's parting the clouds from the sky. It's an ill wind on the other side of the fence. And him so old! You being with him makes him look old. Does it make me look old? You're going to let the bread burn.

Better bury my words. Better to leave, and burn, and wait for a new day. And on the morning of my lucky night . . . !

Better? For what? Not for me.

The good, for a dog, is a bone with meat on it. For a cat the good is little, shy dogs, and many mice. The good for mice is no cats, and a left loaf of bread. The good for birds is no cats, and eggs saved from cats and men. For a horse the good is new grass, and other horses, and a few good men. For man the good is no one thing.

For a sailor, the good is even tides, many ports, and half a wind.

For a cook, the good is unburned meat and the delight of other men.

For one king the good is a kingdom without fools; for another, the good is a kingdom all fools.

For Caesar the good is what makes him Caesar.

For a fool the good is other fools. For other men, the good is what makes fools shy.

But for me, the good is you.

IV

In the early morning a lucky worm would go on sleeping. But what worm sleeps? The egg lies waiting to be a better egg; but it is not to be. What good is the intention of an egg? Time and man "spoil" the egg by making it into another thing — a bird, an omelet.

Soon the cat comes in. It looks at the omelet without any delight at all and goes off.

For me too the day is spoiled. You have gone off. You have even gone off without leaving me any bread. It has taken me a little time to gather what an unlucky wind is blowing. You had led me to look to many good days, green and even days that would propose love and all the little delights that love can save and build into a kingdom — moss, dogs, red eggs . . . But it is not to be. Every day makes new fools out of old ones, and today has chosen me. Like the eggs, my gifts lie broken and not to be gathered up. Is it "Growing old"?

> *A stitch in time,*
>> *A bird in the hand,*
> *A silver lining,*
>> *Wait for no man*

And you can't save an omelet with stitches. You came on all shy with me, when the intention was to take a stick to a dog that had not harmed you. What good are silver words to me when you have as good as left me? Things spoil, burn, are buried — men for one — and words cannot make things new.

And to do it for *him!* When you take another man, take a good one — not a fool, not a mouse, not one who plays cards all day. But was it for him that you did it, for him as him? Wasn't it for all the money that's been left him? You shouldn't have given him the time of day, in other times you would have made him get away at once, but you looked at him and drank with him and took gifts from him and soon were disposed to sleep with him. Did you do this for money — for the meat off dead men's bones? One was taught that "a fool and his money spoil the broth": the words were made for you. And today you propose to me not to put you off, to take love from you as it is given. Don't lie to me always! You're not blind to the poison you've poured into my days. What a sucker you take me for! That's not new — no, and you're getting better at it all the time.

You're looking good — as good as always. Have you been down at the waterside? The wind's burned you — that red mouth. You're going? It's not even six. — Have a good time. Don't take my words to you for ill intentions. My words aren't stones to harm you but fences to make you not harm me. Things will go better for me soon: any tomorrow is better than none, and half a loaf (being with you from time to time) — half a loaf is better than no silver lining.

Come soon — will you come tomorrow and look at my new cards?

Come as soon as you can.

Gone. Day, night: time and tide spoil the broth. You lay down once in the bushes with me. Are you lying down with him, in the bushes on the other side of the road? — Go look? Gathering words one can look at, bush words — ". . . Give it . . . take it . . ." Let it be.

Time has no intentions. It "never sleeps" but it is always sleeping. It will bury tomorrow as it has buried today, without delight, without love. It is not lucky and not unlucky, it does no good and no ill, it is blind and not blind (can it look?), it is old and not old (it never can "be" at all), it is not little and not mighty: but things grow, things spoil, things break, things are built, things are given, things are saved, things are buried, things sleep — and "time" renders the doing and the things done, in nights and days.

V

Words came from you in the morning. One word on the little card said "Rome" — a word that buried my day. You're going to Rome with him. The word made me look up at you as you went away down the road, without having waited for me to come down. It made me give up.

Another gift, and what a gift! Soon you will have met him a dozen times — dozens of times. And every time money is rained on you. Do you play cards? You make money playing cards. Do you look at a horse with love? The horse is gotten for you. And soon

Rome: an intention that, in the words you left me, is a "thing of delight" — thing, thing! Hasn't it been taught him that a dozen gifts spoil one?

You never proposed to me to go away with you. But having money and things is not my gift, and it never will be, no. My gifts to you were little, but given with love. My gifts were few — too few. Half a loaf, unlucky in love.

You never proposed to me to go away, and you aren't doing it today. Couldn't you have done it and left it to me to put off my leaving with you? (With you and him.) A little gift to *me*. You wouldn't have had to wait for my "no" — even to one as blind as me, it's no trick to get what's on the cards.

> *When in Rome*
> > *Few are chosen,*
> *Six of one*
> > *Are another man's poison*

Even one of one. "Too many cooks spoil the bird in the hand," no? And at any time, with you or without you, Rome is not my thing. If one man's meat is the things that are Caesar's, the man must be him and not me.

And soon you'll be rolling down to Rome. Have a good time, go east, go west, but — when in Rome, God disposes! And will dispose of him, could be, with him as old as an oak. No, my days aren't that lucky; but the unturned card is always the sucker's delight.

VI

In the red and silver morning a dead day breaks. New words from you to teach me that, once looked on by you as a king (even too mighty a one, which harms me) — once a king, but broken to a stone, a stick, to be buried in parted days as a dead bird or mouse is buried in the grass. The words that came to you from me in the night you call the poison of love gone dead — you take me to have left the kingdom that was my kingdom with you and to have gone blind, to have grown spoiled — a man spoiled as meat is spoiled.

You will have been taught that you can't teach an old dog without breaking eggs — look at one broken egg. But what will it have taught me? It was an unlucky tide that parted you from me. You are going off into the night. My night. It was not me that did the things to you, but a devil — it has always been one of my tricks never to put off till tomorrow what spoils the broth. But "poison" is too ill a word for me; "spoiled" and "blind" may render it, but never could any poison come to you from me. My words were unlucky. If the winds could have gathered the other words in my mouth, to be saved and poured from the sky . . . ! It is that what you have done is a hell for me, a red burning cloud that has left me burned, and blind.

Blind days are breaking on sailors in hindmost ports. Waiting to go with the tide. You have me in your hand: before you leave on the tide, dispose of the bones you have gathered. But let me come and look at you once before you go, that's all. It's little for you to do. Not that it will be all delight to me — better any time to put off the day of leaving and of leave-taking; but it will be a thing to wait with. A loaf is no gift to a king, but it's a mighty one to a man without meat.

A thing to wait with: for dead days and blind nights. For bread and broth — that's something. Grass will go on growing. Things to do: call the dogs; save time; play cards; lie in the grass; wait for you; go down the road. To look at bushes growing at the road side — bushes that you grew? The road is broken, water gathers in the stones and grass is growing up. One could call the birds in the bushes to drink the water on the stones and look for worms in the stitches of grass. A cat is playing with one unlucky bird's eggs. Another cat lies dead in the road — no, not dead, sleeping; no, not even sleeping: playing with a mouse. The cat soon takes it up. The unlucky mouse in the cat's mouth is not dead.

VII

Rolling clouds gathered in the west, and the wind has been blowing from the west, growing from early morning till night. The clouds came early, little at first, a few silver birds that grew into dogs and horses and parted to be new things, mighty things spoiling for a storm. And all day the growing wind. Wind today, wind tomorrow, and a storm coming. Before night storms the sky looks silver-green. The tide too is coming from the west, with the wind. The night rolls in from the east, and from the west the clouds roll up to meet it. Night is the time when winds gather, and all the other winds are pouring down water and grass. Let the winds blow, let the tide build. Let it rain. It is raining; and blowing; and the tide will soon be pouring onto stones and grass. Water will gather in tide and sky and with it the wind will pave the kingdom of night. The wind will bury the road to the port with the rendered waters.

As for me, it's time to be sleeping. All the devils of the storm cannot spoil my intention of sleeping early.

Night rolled in from the east, clouds from the west rolled up to it — : what were the words of Mark Twain, East is east and west is west and never the two shall meet? Have met! in the wind. In my kingdom the wind is called — no: when it blows at night in the oaks, the wind is called "kingdom"; in the day "road." Not "my" kingdom with me king — king's another man. Sleeping too? Sleeping kings are dead kings. But when a king sleeps, what delights! Stones of time and storm are parted, a new morning sky breaks into the night, and the king's intentions, a little at a time, are built up of silver water, birds, and early clouds. But no king can sleep all night. Kings have been taught that kingdoms are made with poison, it must not be him that is given poison: even when, as kings always must, the king drinks with other men. Kings have been taught that a kingdom is built with broken bones, it mustn't be him that's broken: better that the bones of all the kingdom pave the king's road. Sleeping is soon done for. (And you — don't take poison, not today!) The king gets up, goes to look at the night sky, and the mighty clouds give him delight — another, one-eyed delight.

Night is the time for giving poison to kings, and for man's love. . . . What are the bushes burning on the road? Take no poison — not today!

Soon not sleeping. Wind and burning. When the wind has mighty intentions, call in your horses and dogs. (But love that looks shy is as an oak in the storm. And no wind can break the oaks, not today, not tomorrow.)

Getting up:

Water is pouring from the night sky. What a wind! It's raining from side to side. The wind has buried the road to the port in sky-

and tide-water. The waters meet from time to time and no road is left.

The port sky burns in the night. The storm must be rolling its waters through the port, burying it too. A mighty tide could soon break up the stones of the port. Clouds of water breaking on green stones. . . . When a storm is blowing, let the old sailor in.

Twice the waters have met and rolled down the road. "Dere's a mighty water comin' down de road!" It never rains without breaking eggs, and things play the fool in a storm — water, stones, all the devils, and everything but mice and worms! Better to sleep like them. (Do worms sleep?) Better sleep if one can; and one can.

It could be it's raining worms. (Better worms than poison!) Skies can rain worms, blown from other grasses. And stones — "a day when stones rained from the sky," the silver sky came down: stones are raining down, the dead lie on every road. Dead every which-what. Red dogs drink green water that breaks from the stones.

> *Leave no stone*
> > *Before you leap,*
> *Six of one*
> > *The twain shall meet*

The old dead lie in their silver linings, but the new dead lie in stones and water. You chose the dead; you chose the devils. The water takes old bones from the grass and moss, and silver bones roll in a new tide of stones and water. In my kingdom the dead are not buried, the dead are not buried as in other kingdoms, but are left to spoil in the bushes. In my kingdom the dead are not lucky, are not unlucky. In my kingdom the dead wait without gathering time. In my kingdom the dead have no good intentions and no ill ones, cannot give love, cannot take it; but can spoil and save.

> *Let the dead*
> *Break my bones,*
> *Better than no bread*
> *Sticks and stones*

Old moss lies on unturned bones. You chose the dead and the devils. The dead are not buried in the blind kingdom of worms and water. It is raining, it has rained today all day and all night. It will rain tomorrow and every day. It has always rained. Days of water — the water will drink up the stones. Will it drink the dead? And what of the king? The king isn't dead. (You chose the dead, you chose the devils!) The king is broken and must be given six stitches. The dead can make fools of kings, but to what good? The king will go on sleeping with six stitches and the water and stones. And soon the king will give up sleeping.

The dead of the West are called "God" and "Caesar."

(Have given up sleeping.)

Cats will have been left dead in the road. In the old days one never left dead cats.

When it blows at night, the wind in the oaks is called "kingdom"; in the day, "road."

VIII

Morning, from the east, a mighty sky — an even lining of burning silver clouds, which the new day soon parts.

The storm has spoiled the new grass. It has broken the fences old and new. The kingdom of shy horses lies green and silver in the morning.

The worms have not let the storm spoil their day. Look at their comings and goings! What are they gathering? What's bread for a worm?

And as for my bread — no bread for me today. What to do? Anything, that's what. The road to Hell is better than no bread.

But the break of day proposes new intentions. Look: a loaf of bread has been left for me, by you — you! — and a few words: ". . . Storm played tricks . . . Words coming from him that were ill words to me . . . Fools . . . No road to Rome, not with him!"

Delight breaks from me as birds break from morning clouds. The unlucky time is done for. Blind days burn away. Time and tide will bury their dead.

When did you come and leave the things, the words and the bread? The gift of the loaf you made was worth many words of love. When did you come in, with me not sleeping? On what night tide, from what other side of the sky —

The clouds have parted and lie before the wind.

The dog in the bushes — dead? sleeping?

What good bread you make! And you have not left me. Love disposes of cats and kings, but a good stitch never parts. Can any man be as lucky? That unturned card was a one-eyed king.

And at night you will come and take me to you. You will not

have come too soon. The dead were waiting for me, might have come soon, waiting, paving the road that leads into their kingdom with the green mosses of unlucky delight (delight of sleeping, of going blind, of being one with the night). When you are with me, their poison will be poured away.

IX

The new fence was broken in the storm. How the wind must have blown to break it — to blow it down. The fence lay on one side all day. Horses gathered on one side and on the other; the horses came up to the fence and looked at it and at the other horses; but none went onto the others' grass. Today men will come and put the oak fence up and make it as good as new.

The wind is gone, the mighty wind (one to make Caesar wait for a day): today the wind is even, an early wind to be drunk in.

Soon going down: to be met with another gift from you — a dozen red eggs. Gifts should be given with the intention of delight (and red eggs are even better). Better than all is the gift of gifts, you, none other, coming to me down road and grass.

You had come to me at night, you came to me in the early morning; and all the day went on in delight. A few words once and for all of him, of you and him, of you and me and him:

"When you were going with him . . ."

"Don't! It's done with."

"It's done with — but isn't anything left of the love you had for him?"

"It wasn't love — the intention of love, that's all. My one love is for you, it will never be for another. With him it never could have been."

"You waited for love to come, it never comes, it has to be made — take it from me. Have a little bread?"

"All the days gone for nothing — spoiled."

"Rome wasn't built without breaking eggs."

"But for him! It wasn't worth it."

"What did the storm do to him — not a man of mighty waters?"

"No — but one of many waters: always going off . . . What made me a sucker for him? A sucker!"

"Never should've let you go off with him — 'Never let a sucker even break eggs,' as the teaching goes."

"The storm made me lucky. It taught me what to look for in him: money, and that's all."

"'A fool and his money, sailors take warning' — "

"But 'A stitch in time, sailor's delight'!"

"You can play the card with me today — today, and any day!"

That was that.

Morning is not done when you propose to teach me the love of mice. Love of cat, dog, and horse, good — but love of mouse?

"The shy mouse that never looks at the sky . . . Wait."

You leave a road of bread for the mice — many roads: a Rome of sticks and moss. The sticks are disposed to make fences at the side of the roads, which are paved with the moss, with the bread broken on it. Soon mice come from grasses and stones, one at a time, and go down the roads gathering the bread: little silver kings.

When you have taught me mouse love, you propose worms. Worms! Mice and worms may meet in the grass; and mice and worms may never have to drink; but to me a mouse is to a worm as day is to night. You teach me, "The intentions of worms are few but mighty. The night kingdom of worms can break all things. Mighty stones lie on worms and do not harm them. When one is harmed, a worm has a trick of breaking into six or nine and growing into new worms. Today's worm is tomorrow's dozen . . ."

Worm love is left to another day.

When bread and meat were done with, you took me into the kingdom of clouds and birds: down a new road. Even a fool would have taken delight at being on it, never away from the water, and all green on the other side — oaks and bushes breaking with green. Few grasses have had time to grow on the road, but in the stones acorns are disposing green suckers. You lead me into the oaks and bushes, on old sticks green with moss, on off-red mosses lying on stones from which silver water breaks. You teach me that oaks can have moss on all sides. You teach me to look for bird's eggs, and to part the eggs from the birds without harming one and the other. (Six eggs lay burning-red on moss.) You led me on till, parting the grasses, you looked onto the water that lies to the east. No one had taught me that one could get to it on the new road.

Little clouds wait in the sky; other clouds lie even with the water: no wind. A stick from my hand takes time going away in the water. You let one hand lie in the water — should one go in? You have other intentions.

You lead me down the road to look at horses that can be got for little money — no "My kingdom for a horse" for you! On the grass rolling away from the road, many horses are calling to one another.

Choosing a horse is new to me. What has been taught to me of horses? That a horse has one good side; that when you call a dog i comes, when you call a cat it may come, but a horse comes to you without calling.

A red horse takes one of the fences twice. A little horse is coming up to the road — it's taking the road fence! Don't let it get away! A man is coming to get him, stick in hand. (That wouldn't do me any good: taking a stick to a horse would spoil my day.)

It is you that chooses the horse, and what a horse! You propose a little money, wait for a time, and take me away. Tomorrow you will come and you'll get the horse.

Night like day breaks from the east like a silver egg. Many other days are to come. What will new days and nights propose to you and me? The delight of sleeping in the morning — of sleeping all day, lying down in the morning and getting up at night. You will teach me to play cards, you will teach me to grow old. You can take me egg-rolling. You can take me down to the water with a dozen worms. You can teach me "Save a sailor!" You will teach me every night to look to the morning. You will give me a hand. Saving a little money would be a good thing. You will make things new, and choose green linings to go with the grass and red ones not to. You will take me as God made me. You will lie down with me. You will let time do its tricks. And, from one day to another, one-eyed delight will go on playing with old silver birds.

X

A storm one day made the meat spoil (not the mighty storm, another one, when many days had come and gone). The meat had spoiled:

you had been unlucky in not putting it away with a west wind blowing. With a west wind, worms in meat grow better, and it soon goes all silver and green. And even to you, meat worms are no delight — maybe you once had worms? No, you're a cook, and worms can never be a delight to a cook. That is what is good with omelets: never a worm.

The wind had spoiled the meat, and with it your delight in making meat, broth, bread, omelets, and other things. Once you had a cook. ("What did he leave for?" "Too many cooks are soon parted.") The day had come, you gathered, to have another.

At the time, the cooks of many kingdoms had chosen the port down the road for a mighty gathering; and you took me with you to choose a new cook from the ones that had come.

The port was as it had been before — the storm had broken it up, but it had been built new. Not many sailors had been taken by the storm. The tide can play tricks with sailors, as can the wind, but on the day of the storm, wind and tide led many sailors into port in time.

What tide and wind are to sailors, meat and broth are to cooks: and in port the words "meat" and "broth" were in every mouth (and "egg" too).

(Were any of the cooks sailors, any of the sailors cooks? To be at once a cook and a sailor is to be twice king.)

Choosing a cook is a mighty thing. Time can make even fools into good cooks, but it is better to have a good one from the word go. You must have money — money can make and break kings, and it may even get one a cook; but a *good* cook? A good cook can dispose of kings. You must get the cook's love too, with one thing and another. The love of a good cook is better than any king's — it is worth the kingdom of God.

But for cooks good and ill, money is good to have. "Too many cooks have a silver lining" are the words in which you rendered it. But you went on (when many cooks had not taken up what you were proposing), " 'Too many cooks' *has* a silver lining, too: six of one would be better than no bread!" Too many cooks, but few are chosen — or choose. It was night before one was disposed to come away with you.

Many days came and went, good ones; till today, when the cook let the meat burn. The cook was sleeping, and unturned meat soon burns. Sleeping — in the daytime? You do not have to be taught that cooks drink: a cook may always have to have water at hand, but it isn't for drinking. Sleeping in the daytime, and sleeping all night too, with the birds and the other cooks. You had been ill-disposed to him before, and your words to him were unlucky ones — calling him a fool and proposing that good cooks were dead cooks. The cook went all red and soon was gone; and all the money you had given him was gone with the wind . . . with the cook . . . Too many cooks wait for no man.

The meat has burned — and red meat is good for the drinking man; but save the bones for broth and the broth for tomorrow's meat. Bones make for good broth, and good broth makes a mighty man. Put in any old meat you have, too — it can render good broth.

You give me the broth and make an omelet. You teach me that it should be made without water, and that when making it a good thing is to roll it. It's time for bread and eggs. Save a little bread to gather up what will be left of the omelet.

You have made better omelets before.

Dead cooks do not make better cooks — that is what the day has taught me.

XI

Once burned,
> *Leave no stone unturned.*
Twice shy,
> *Let sleeping dogs lie.*

Days have come and will come, todays and tomorrows, todays paved with tomorrows and with days that are gone. The tomorrows lie on today as the dead do. It is time to give them up.

As cats gather mice, as ports gather sailors, you gather old intentions. Every day you gather me and put me away. You have called me a king, but you look on me as the bones of today that will soon be dead, you put the day away with me, the "king." Don't take the king for the kingdom. The kingdom is today.

Tomorrow can be intention, but today does not wait: it is delight or not. The morning is the one morning, or no morning. Delight as to the grass-gathering horse. The dog's mouth cannot put off the time when it will take up the bone. Cards are given to me, to you. Every card takes a trick, and one lucky card is worth a kingdom.

Today breaks into little winds, roads, clouds. The wind that comes from the tide of clouds is gathering intentions, of silver days and of storms. Don't wait for it. The time that will come "soon" has come today. All roads "take it with you." Tomorrow is for the birds — the early birds that look away to tomorrow. But the early bird must come down.

Oaks are growing and gathering their linings of green. Moss gathers on oaks, on sticks of dead oak, on stones. Grass grows and soon is dead, and grows new, and the dead grass is taken into the kingdoms of birds, mice, and worms. In the morning, sticks are being gathered and broken. It's time to go into the day. Sticks are gathered at the water side, and dead oak that makes for good burning burns. Dead grass too burns at the road side.

It is time to go blind into the day. Let the blind dog that you led lead you. Dead times grow in the grass, in the oaks (the dead are parted from none), but from them oaks and grass grow new. Time to give up one thing and another (but take one gift from me). Let everything go. Let everyone go — let the cook be gone! The time has come to let it all go. Give what you can. Put silver money in the blind man's hands. (But money is a little gift, and gathers little men. "For a cook a gift of silver, for a sailor a gift of time, for a good man a gift of love.") Give bones to the old dog, give broth and meat to the old man lying at the side of the road. Spoil the mighty horse that has broken down. But for you, take the day that is today; and the night with it.

Red bones break in the old dog's mouth.

It will be night all too soon. In the west, birds will part the lining of day. The day will break down, and clouds burn for it.

It will soon be night, and soon tomorrow. The cards will lie unturned. The horses, having drunk, will sleep. Mice will take to their little roads. The sleeping logs die. The birds are disposed in the oaks for the night. And the worms — what do worms do in the night, blind things? Do worms gather when parting meat from bone?

Night comes, time to make broth and meat. You cannot let everyone in. But let the dog in, and the cat, and me. The kingdoms will soon be sleeping, for tomorrow. And for tomorrow — for tomorrow bury the dead things of today. Bury and burn the always-old things; pour off the rest:

Burn a dozen and one cards. Bury a few acorns. Pour off the even tide. Bury the poison-birds and the cook's lucky dog and cat.

Burn the grass devils and half the night. Pour off the ill waters. Burn the sides and linings of things, the cloud men, and the better Other. Pour off the rolling wind. Bury the little tricks, the unlucky sailor, the stone mouth, and the mice dead from poison. Bury the loaf storms. Burn the bone fences. Burn the oak sticks and another day. Bury the old horse and the unturned moss. Pour off the eggs. Bury the sleeping hands, the green breaks, and the hindmost road. Burn delights and intentions (the twain) and their time-bushes. Pour off the fool's words and the others. Burn the nine gods and every gift, the good stitches and the new suckers. Bury Rome and Caesar, the kingdom and the king, and the hell in the red west. Pour off the early morning. Burn the new port, the oak sticks, and the one-eyed sky. Bury any love. Burn the silver east. Bury meat and omelets, and pour off the mighty broth.

The burning fences make red stitches in the lining of the sky. Red clouds dispose the night.

II

The American Experience: Stories to Be Read Aloud

THE WAY HOME

Imagination moves by angles, along a black line inscribed on a white ground that is itself bordered by blackness. The mind rests when it comes to identifiable objects athwart or alongside this line: chewable wood pellets, for instance, or a woman catching minnows. The imagination then faces, after many other obstacles, a choice it cannot avoid: whether to engage the identifiable object — that is, face its identity as a clear or coded sign that will help the imagination round the next angle — or to accept it as no more than an occasion for rest, something to lean an elbow on while drawing fresh and not necessarily metaphorical breath. For instance, the woman catching minnows may be simply an image of pleasantly inconsequential country work, hardly significant to the passerby except as a pretext for pastoral-minded relaxation (an effect heightened by the skirts drawn up in her right hand above her bright, reflected knees); or she may turn to him and speak.

One class of objects provides the imagination with peculiar confusion and, perhaps, opportunity: the class of objects that can be recognized but not named, that strike the voyager as having every right to claim a place in the real world (the real world of the imagination) but whose context he cannot remember or conceive of. Think of a rectangular box whose six sides, made of composition board, are separated from each other by spaces five-eighths of an inch across. No magnet, twine, or loosened screw connects them, and yet the box keeps its shape in front of our eyes without straining our reason or our belief.

Can we associate objects such as this with the moment in which desire is conceived? Are they desire's catalysts or its companions? In the real world, the real world of the imagination, the appearance of such objects operates, or allows the voyager to operate, a reversal of elements: for example, day will turn to night, and not necessarily the night of dreams. More simply, darkness will replace light, as though the white ground, out of some sublimely appropriate courtesy, had surrendered to the blackness bordering it. No loss is felt at this moment, and no confusion. The reversal and the surrender produce, it is true, a surprisingly new context, but clearly this context has been created in response to an imperious need. The voyager knows that in the reality of his imagination he cannot hope to understand his need except through an exploration of the context that has been created for this very purpose. So he has no sense of confusion. He may have a sense of desire, and of the fear that goes with desire (that school of flitting minnows). More probably, he has little sense of anything except the darkness that gives the new object such frosty brightness.

At times objects will distract and finally disappoint him. They will give rise to graceful or interesting explanations. Thus a group of inanimate, irregular solids will be seen through a screen of swaying vines, and the traveler, who has after all not slept for days or years or even since the time of his birth, will rest his eyes (and his nose, his tongue) on these vines, becoming ridiculously pleased with himself when he discovers they are not vines at all but the little green clusters of bastard toadflax or the slender blackish stalks of some fern he remembers from moister, warmer climes. He forgets the chewable wood pellets.

Mr. Maltmall had spent the greater part of his life, perhaps every moment since his birth, in shadowy, imaginary voyage. He flitted precariously at the hub of time's wheel like a hummingbird motionlessly voyaging at the center of a spoked, nameless flower. The spokes of the flower sharpened his engagement with life, hovering pointedly on the periphery of his vision like the figures on a clock face or the circle of constellations on an astrological calendar. They reminded him that he had committed himself to a ceremonial of limited duration, so that while they did not confine him, out of the knowledge of his finiteness he kept his enthusiasm at a whirring pitch, like a partisan mounting guard on a quiet night in territory occupied by the oppressor, like a mandarin rewriting salutary laws that neglect and misrule have left a shambles.

He held himself straight, with a slight bend of alertness in his knees. Not lean or fat, he gave an impression of despondent strength, with his wide, bent shoulders. His beard, once thoroughly black, had turned brownish and was mixed with sparse white hairs. When he was offended, his lips and the tip of his nose looked blue against his florid face. He gestured and walked with considered slowness, as if not to offend in turn. He spoke in a harsh, broad voice pitched agreeably low.

Sometimes, as he considered deeds, prospectuses, contracts, an apparition would form in the chinks of the print, delineated by the cascade of spaces flowing through terms of payment and mortgage allowances. (The words by no means bored him, lively as they were with promises of building, exchange, and newly roofed lives.) Amidst these technicalities first a white haze, then a white possibility emerged in the background of the page: a waterside of reeds and redwing blackbirds, sun-warmed shallows glittering beyond, apparently roiled by the swoop of an oar — but it was too shallow there for an oar, something else was being dragged through the fertile water, a pole, or the bared foot of a wader. Beyond the reeds, beyond the fine bunched type, Mr. Maltmall assembled an event out of whiteness and light, the way a starwatcher connects a constellation from dispersed bunches of stars.

The scene he had thus encountered or constructed in his attentive, imaginary travels provoked a sense in him less of desire than of hopeful curiosity. He felt that something new had been promised him, new, agreeable, and perhaps illuminating. The promise immediately restored his gift for noticing small, attractive anomalies in the course of his ordinary life. At lunch his place was set with a fork to the left of his plate, another fork to the right of his plate. On his way to the beach, a short clothesline sagged inexplicably with the weight of a single stiff, fluffy diaper.

Some of his friends were already smacking a ball over the volleyball net set up on a level area of off-white sand. "Walt the Malt!" they cried when they saw him. He took his place among them. His

teammates appreciated the sharp accurate smashes that he made using the outside of his fist. He played willingly enough, although he was never completely absorbed by the game. He liked best the moments when he tossed the ball high in the air to serve and looked up into the hazy summer sky. That afternoon, turning away from the net after a point-winning smash, he saw a boy and girl down the beach hitting a shuttlecock back and forth in high, slow parabolas and wished that he could join them.

The whipped paddle, the shuttlecock's lazy flight: real play. After the team changed sides, the children were constantly in view. The sun drooped behind dunes; one swipe sailed the white-plastic feathers into its tilted rays, which seemed to catch and hold them at the apogee of their flight. Walt was reminded of a high note near the end of a solo by John Coltrane, sustained with sweetly inhuman intensity. The volleyball hit Walt on the nose. He clenched his eyes. In blackness, lines of brilliant light streamed outwards from a twirling, shadowy center that he longed to cling to, at least until his nose forgave him. He wiped his eyes. Bouncing from his face, the ball had been retrieved by an alert teammate. He had not lost the point. It was his turn to serve.

Subsiding twinges in his buffeted eyes looped red, readable strands against the gold-showered sky: an old woman with a staff was prodding three sheep towards a marketplace. He blinked and tapped the ball far into the opposite court. The red scene, quickly gone, recalled to him the morning's waterside apparition. It had been very different. The red scene held no promise, he knew it at once to be only a relic of some childhood story, of no use to him now even as a place to rest and breathe. The battledore partners were calling it a day.

The air cooled, and evening cooled the tones around him —

pale gray sand, blue-gray ocean, black-and-whitening beach grass, the volleyball black when tossed against the sky. Walt Maltmall: he silently pronounced his name with bitterness and contempt. Playing ball looked to him like playing at still-growing childhood; and he resembled rather the aged, disheveled, waddling gull that was methodically exploring litter on the emptying beach. After his friends said goodbye, he shut his eyes, making literal his feeling that he was losing his sight, his feeling that the only living sensation in him was a thoroughly blind urge to follow something — something that was running away from him, something tender that might be caught, torn to pieces, eaten, held against his tearless cheeks. He hated this urge, which had the reddish blackness of rage, and hated his self-hatred. Stars faded against the maroon depths of his eyelids.

Fading or not, the stars restored a sense of space outside the restricted corridor of his imagined pursuit. He considered the new space opening around him, soon huge enough, and the objects it presented as they slid past him. He saw a baby fastened to the nipple of an adolescent girl's breast, poking it compulsively and regularly with tiny fists. The capital letter S stood alone and high against a landscape of pale orchards and vine-covered hillslopes. A solitary joker in cap and bells lay on a wooden table painted a brownish shade of maroon. His father was showing him how to thread a rod used for fly fishing. An ad he had once placed in the Sunday *Times* displayed a photograph of a thirty-room shingle house with broad lawns surrounding it. Seen from behind, a young woman dexterously plugged and unplugged the connections of a hotel switchboard. A cake encrusted with green rock candy proposed a bright red plum at its center.

There is no object so soft but that it makes a hub of the wheeled universe. There is no shadow so slow but that it makes a wing of the wheeling soul. There is no thought so precarious but that it makes a word of the drenched shadow. There is no pit so shallow but that it

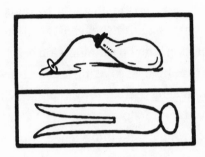

makes a chasm of the sensible intelligence. There is no drink so wet but that it makes a desert of the dying voice. There is no sonatina so short but that it makes a fluency of the chartered streets. There is no brood so scattered but that it makes a hearth of the dying miser. There is no man, no woman so lost but that she makes a goal of the attentive will. No book so sold but that it makes an expectation of the obsolescent barman. No dish so bland but that it makes a lesson of the deserving dog. No Walt so Malt but that he makes a shadow of the universal wheel.

And that woman, that young woman picking mallows, if that is what she's doing — in a vague way, he dreaded banishing her to the hillsides, where he would no longer hear the fretting of her corduroyed inner thighs. He had reached an angle of his black line and was afraid of becoming stuck there. He did not want to rely on her to help him around the angle, to turn his journeying gaze down the next stretch of black band. What he somewhat less vaguely imagined he had to do to negotiate the turn was to step away from what lay in front of him, to turn his back on it and then keep turning until he had swung around into the direction of the next straight passage. He imagined her helping him if he chose this more extensive but more yielding shift onto his new course. She would broaden or even complete his intended revolution by providing an angle of darkness equal to his own darkness. Addressing it, he might have to relinquish breathing completely, his mouth buried in blackish fern, his nose pinched shut in her pleasurable native grasp. Such symmetry made no sense, it meant not vaguely but precisely dark to dark, his eyes (whether open or shut) also stifled by beach balls — hers. He followed her into the hills.

Deep into the night, he told himself that he had no excuse not to be at work on time. His imaginary journeying demanded actual common-or-garden movement, not sitting around contemplating the situation. Perceptions came as accessories to keeping appointments, to reading the fine print. Movement meant shuttling day after day between familiar places, which all the same were tinged with a kind of mental dye if they promised to coincide with his secret itinerary of desire. It had been the same during his childhood when places to go meant the rooms of his parents' apartment or at most the buildings on his grandmother's farm. His grandmother had built a sheepfold with a protective cupola over it and had painted the cupola with green polka dots scattered across a coal-black field. Walt as a boy knew the minute he saw it that the covered fold would be a refuge; and he soon settled himself inside it in moments of neglect, crouching and daydreaming among stuffy ewes and lambs, many of them shorn and ticketed for sale and slaughter.

Was there truly a black angled line, inscribed on a white background, along which he perceptibly moved? Or was he still at his point of departure, the readiness of departure forming the substance of his life rather than any calculably real advance? He pictured himself as a runner in an everlasting crouch, one foot on the starting block; or launched into a first stride, neither foot touching the ground and destined never to touch the ground. Whom was he racing against? All those he knew stood behind him or along the nearby sidelines, while those he imagined knowing were waiting on the far side of the finish line.

A foot straining with the promise of motion: can that ever be called motion? Shouldn't the foot disappear entirely in the swift blurred revolution of the runner's stride (and there was no stride either, only the race)? Walt said to himself and to some others, "I say that's what it's all about." Then why did he insist on feeling like a mere foot, and sometimes like a shoe, full of the best and most useful intentions?

He lay down in the moist, black ferns. He had hoped to reach a lake, but he'd stumbled into this marsh in the darkness, which fell so quickly these mid-September days. He didn't really mind. The marsh mud was like lake-bottom mud in its warm clayiness and its sweet, mulchy smell. He wiggled his fingers and toes into it, his nose, his pelvis, and at last his tongue. (He expected the mud to taste shittily bitter; it proved almost bland.) He bit down into the clay. He thought: now stop breathing, keep burrowing your face into this muck, let yourself go, let it all go. Would that be so bad? The mud still kept some of the sun's warmth, its squelchiness was consolation made matter. Where else is there to go? And if I go there, how will I explain the way I look?

He nestled in the mud bed like a shoe tree inside a closeted black shoe. He knew he could not stay there. He had lost the least intention of motion, of travel, he had forgotten the daylight and the succession of amusing days. He became aware of this himself because against the dark lining of his eyelids he saw nothing but mudlike darkness. He was enjoying himself. He found it ecstatically soothing to be able to look at what could not be called nothing, since there was a blankly black something there, but a something shorn of every physical and metaphysical detail, a mass of empty soft flat indifferent darkness. When he was through enjoying himself (a moment he had to pick willfully), he stood up out of the mud and returned to the living world of his imagination.

So much remains to be told, so much remains to be disguised in order to be told. The image of the black shoe cannot be right, even to describe a condition of solitude. There is never a condition of solitude. It is as if a cat arrived in a town and discovers that it has become a ghost town. Signs along the main street indicate that the town is now in the power of mouse ghosts, who threaten all cats with suffering and death. And the newcomer cat is duly made to suffer and die. He becomes a ghost in turn; he is thus able to reassert his predominance over the mice who had so gleefully persecuted him. So Walt Maltmall, glittering blackly with the muck of oblivion, returned with no apparent stealth to his bungalow and breakfast.

A moment occurs in the dawn twilight when the oppression of darkness and the oppression of light are symmetrical, although our dread of light is greater because we know that is what now threatens us. At that moment Walt diverted himself with abstract concepts, like dialectic, process, or signification. These concepts became or replaced the familiar wayside objects of the category "things to lean against." To emerge from this state of abstraction, Walt needed certain omens: a red knot, a patch of windlessness, an agreeable stench, something conspicuously if loosely recurrent, like the displacements of a lawnmower outside the deli he was now passing. He could conveniently adapt what he came across (the knot could be one in a painted board) but he needed to focus on these reassuringly tangible things in order to realign the disordered self he had knowingly left to one side when he resorted to generalities.

Walt was modern enough in his way. He knew that the money he made was no more than worldly acknowledgement of his commitment to playing the work game. He disliked poker because, when he played the play game, he resented having his decisions judged according to the same principle. (He also hated losing.) He knew perfectly well that work and play were fictions, mirror-faceted shoes on the runner's feet; whereas knees, nude and evasive, promised more genuine significances.

But when Walt began looking for omens, he found his awareness obfuscated by anticipations of matters and people to be dealt with during his forthcoming day — matters of money and pride. The anticipations then revived memories: memories not of material events but of old fantasies, which replayed themselves as black-and-white movies in an utterly dark, undefined space. Once, taking the form of an adolescent girl, he opens the door of the guest room and finds his grandparents in gravely ecstatic copulation. The young girl does not know whether to shut the door as softly as she opened it or to drape herself like a film of cream across their grizzled bodies. Their grizzled hair and skin have stirred her by reminding her of the skin on the faces of ewes as they entered a domed fold at twilight. In another movie he finds himself in a junkyard littered with battered although almost new pie tins and old knives of widely differing sizes but identical design. This movie has an obsessive voice-over: "The very word is like a knell, the very word is like a knell . . ."

As he approached home the needed omens manifested themselves. When he reached his front door he spent a moment looking through the peephole, which offered him a slightly blurred but undistorted view of the interior, with at its center the ball on the newel post, reflective as a mirror, shadowy as a closed eye. He was looking forward to his breakfast, after possibly a quick washup: frozen tangerine juice, Del Monte peaches, instant coffee with a drop of Carnation milk in it (remember not to cheat and suck a delectable jet out of the punctured can), a cigarette between coffees, the smoke at his elbow rising tenuous and straight towards the ceiling. He longed to have a mutt that would sidle up to him at such moments and lie across his feet. He was aware at the same time of bristling with aversions to all the pure and impure dog breeds of the world. He opened the front door and entered his home contentedly. He stopped to consider his barely distinguishable reflection in the varnished globe on the newel post: it looked like his memory movies before they coalesced into objects limp or stiff.

He took off his mud-caked shoes, washed off the mud, filled their insteps with crumpled newspaper, and set them out on the west deck to dry. He straightened up too quickly after putting them down, so that the blood drained out of his head and he had to lean on the

railing of the deck. Shutting his eyes, he had a glimpse in the maroon darkness of the woman at the waterside, the minnow fisher, standing up to her ankles in the glittering pond. She raised her skirt to her hips, pointed her right leg a little to the side, and loosed a sunspangled quivering shaft into the roiled water at her feet. And ever shalt thou yearn. At least he hoped to. Or rather he expected to look forward to — he mentally and quickly made the correction since he knew hope to be no more than a barb on the hook of desire; he had no intention of ending up like a trout on his father's line, even if he knew that soon he would be considerately released.

Miss Minnower! She probably got along with all kinds of dogs, knowing when to leash and unleash them, when to let them chase cats and when to let the cats chase them. If only she would look back, cast wide her arms, let her frizzled hair fall behind her ears and show her face to him and the generous sun! Teeth and all.

He knew that he must move on from this scene. It too now belonged to the past, the past of expectations. Nothing wrong with that. Halfway through his peaches he sensed that light had begun

shining on the path in front of him. The view remained one of gloom
and murk, but he was fairly sure of a division of the dark grayness
into lighter elements withdrawing right and left and blacker elements
starting to concentrate in the center of the picture, soon to become a
way, his way. He sat and waited for more light, or more clarity, as
though waiting for a roll of the dice in Monopoly, which as a boy he
had played addictively if never with much intelligence.

He did not have to wait long. In the dissolving grayness a black
band led straight ahead of him towards the next angle. He could
even see what awaited him there: a familiar scene, a country fair, in
the midst of which he noticed a broad, slowly turning wheel connected with some game of chance, a wheel segmented according to
the succession of the constellations, with what seemed to be a cap-
tive plastic hummingbird fluttering in a shaft of air expelled from the
center of the wheel. He had barely started down the path when he
felt a light tap on the side of his head. Looking round, he discovered
his beloved grandmother in her red cloak and pointed red hat. She
was leading him and his fellows to the fair, prodding him considerately behind his ticketed ear, leading them to the country fair past
freshly winnowed fields.

TEAR SHEET

Justice has been done, said the occupied girl, withdrawing an icepick from the neck of the occupant. Elsewhere interpretations differ: does equality mean equal rights, or one law for all? If that is the case, who should pay?

As she stepped out of the shower, her foot slipped an inch to one side.

Through the plate glass window of a café he watched a man pick up his order: a hot dog, slipped into a cylinder of bread previously impaled on a hot spike. Mild hunger briefly warmed his throat.

He knew the places where he had lived: the modest suburb of a regional capital and, summers, his grandmother's farm. He knew the places where he wanted to live: a tree-lined street in the national capital and, off-seasons, Cap d'Antibes, if it was still there. He lived now among given forms, not because of them, not in spite of them. The chicken factory had been sited on the drained swamp. Mail arrived with gratifying promptness because sorting and delivery were awarded as prizes to schoolchildren. The roof of the volleyball court could not be reached even when he smashed the ball straight upwards with all his might, into the darkness from which no sound returned, only the ball.

Yesterday someone had questioned him about the availability of land past the city limits, enough for a five-room house and a garden plot.

If only he had known! Not so long ago it would have been easy to claim a chunk of the market, not in rolled glass, of course, but in something like fibrous-rooted begonias. Then dreams could have come true. His favorite dream was a gift to the community: sun conditioning, or optical fiber galore. In the walls of every building in town, little or big, he would have installed thousands of yards of optical-fiber rods that could bend light and conduct it, piping sunshine into the last windowless or buried space. Tanned faces and camellias burgeoning in workshops, in partitioned offices, in underground hobby-rooms! Sunlight in staircases, in emergency stairwells, in the rest-rooms of movie theaters, in low-ceilinged corridors where eight doors face eight other doors, in police-station cells, in bakery basements with their steel ovens and dusted walls, in the depths of banks where massive doors are clamped shut. Sunlight in the workpits of garages when encrusted metal roofs them, sunlight in the backrooms of shops — key shops, shirt shops, shoe repair shops, bicycle shops, computer shops, antique shops, household-appliance shops. Sunlight in rooms where desk lamps, lipstick holders, or spiral notebooks are assembled by indefatigable hands; in the hotel bar between the lobby and the dining area; in the emergency wards strewn with blood-reddened lint. Sunlight in elevators. He remembered outside elevators on turn-of-the-century buildings in his home town, rising and descending through the day as though the work of construction had never ended.

Down the avenue, his umbrella sailing above those around him, he walked past a beautician's, a travel agency, a bank, his own real-estate office. Along the back walls of the warmly lighted interiors an uninterrupted landscape displayed haunting colors: spruce-covered slopes reflected in a sky-blue lake; the beaches of Ceylon; on one of the town's squares, children riding a merry-go-round; Versailles. He crossed a neighborhood of shops, then several blocks of middle- to low-priced, ten- to twelve-storey housing until, via the underpass, he reached the bus depot.

She was waiting in the cafeteria. In her impeccable uniform she shook him with freshened yearning. He had walked through the chilling rain to develop his sadness.

That morning she had learned where she'd been posted. The bus would take her to the airport. She kissed the palms of Walt Maltmall's hands and told him to keep quiet. Before she stepped onto the bus, he realized that if the sun were shining they would cast a single shadow across the asphalt.

The bus will take her south out of town, past the detached and the semidetached, past the shopping center and its prodigiously flourishing conifers, past the soccer fields, past the white sign enamelled with the town's ancient name (now inscribed in her forever), at whose very foot a tractor track swerves in a rounded right-angle turn away into the sodden vastness.

He himself had nowhere to go. He was already there.

LETTERS FROM YEREVAN

They, the others, see no problem. Each woman, or human, presents a desire not only real but specific; each provides the one vehicle that can convey them to a particular, namable haven.

"I want a dead end all my own," you write. What if it's the other way round? And who is that "you" speaking? Pure slobber, as well as a sniffing backwards in some sort of nasal retch, because of one dead male. From low-lying clouds, slim but apparently of three-dimensional solidity, hidden hands strew flakes of foil to mask the proceedings. Who is that creature, or person, shaking the struts of a crib, spewing flakes of hot foam into the indifferent atmosphere?

The tragic overture, sung by a mezzo-soprano named Cecilia to the accompaniment of an Iberian mezzo-piano, slowly introduced us, in spite of her pain, to the notion of the arabesque: a serpentine, actively moving line that seizes on motives in the general panorama and mobilizes them. This produces unexpected feelings that are hard to explain but become — also inexplicably — unquestionably precise. If, as another example, you are reading about Grieg's painful troubles with sexual prophylaxis and how his pain led to Cecilia's own, which made the rendering of her song so compelling, you do not have to be familiar with Grieg's music, or with Cecilia's life (her family name was Zens or Kenz), to project against the curtainlike haze of your dreamery a sequence that you can identify, interpret, and react to.

Is your pleasure in this comparable to the thrust of "their" infatuation? Please detach yourself from the urge to make such comparisons. You are far from Troy or Ithaca, and nearer a place like Elmira. An actor of talent passes you on the street. What is he doing in this out-of-the-way place? You turn around, follow him for a few steps, long enough to touch the imaginary hump on his back. Except that at that moment, noticing a coin or a flyer on the pavement in front of him, he stops and bends over, with the result that your hand gropes in empty air above his hips. He glimpses you from below, through his bent, slightly spread legs. Straightening up, he smiles, says "Sorry" and hands you the flyer: an advertisement, which you read, for a novel about the demise of a legendary hero of finance, told from the point of view of his disconsolate baby hound.

Is it conceivable that a Paraguayan peddlar of second-hand duds could needlessly spoil his friendship with the top money-shooter of America? This hero turns out to be a heroine, "all heart," according to the novelist, "although I never actually met her." The novelist speaks of her "fatal sentimentality" and compares her to a skater inscribing one fine straight line across a frozen pond, suddenly touched by the thought of creatures trapped beneath the ice and then veering towards a spring-fed cove: the ice fractures and crackles like bullet-pocked plate glass, and through the tracery foiling the blackness around the yet blacker but still tumultuous hole can be distinguished the noses, pressed up against the ice, of forlorn rabbits, chipmunks, and voles. From the skate-rental concession scrapy strains of "Falling in Love with Love" are blown across the pond where, says the author, "skaters I actually spoke to" explain the comparative object of the metaphor as a case of unrequited passion — that of the financier heroine for a Japanese *haute couture* mogul, who agreed to create and market a perfume that bore her name; but that was it. The fissures in the ice snap occasionally as the frost intensifies; and when darkness falls, the hole at their center itself freezes into a starlike spot of scrumbled light.

What had the peddlar to do with this? He had had the idea; had raised himself from his world of white nylon shirts, pisco, and hangnails to a level where he could arrange the meeting of heroine and mogul; had counseled her — since the mogul, who liked to be called Ginger, had been tabbed as a likely homosexual — to dress in male attire. It so happened that for their first meeting Ginger himself wore one of his own creations, a black linen chuckaround frock, but he only did this for business-talk effect, not from sexual predisposition. The deal was cut in a whirl of emotional confusion and disappointment. Ginger was in fact drawn to demurely feminine women, certainly not to one in a Mets uniform, with all her sumptuous hair tucked inside her cap. The deal went through, the mogul left subsequent negotiations to assistants, and the heroine never forgave the peddlar. She found little consolation among the rabbits and voles.

Her name was Taylor. She used taxis, always tipping the drivers to drive slowly, and never bought a car. She listened to Cecilia's performance of Grieg with tearless compassion, her pale fingers barely pressing the stripes along her thighs. To the invitation of her observant dinner companion, a "foundation president whom I actually interviewed on the phone," she gave the simplest of assents. She deserved better than to have her story smirched by the strolling soles of Elmira.

On the corner of a notable intersection, a tan, middling-size dog is performing an elaborate gymnastic act that culminates in a double flip. Traffic slows down to watch, pedestrians stop for a minute or two. Most onlookers go off shaking their heads to express a mixture of emotions in which pitying disapproval overcomes admiration. This attitude is mistaken: if they watched more closely, they would see that the dog enjoys performing and is elated by his competence. Beyond this observation, I'm not sure how and why the dog appears on this corner and so on this page. One clue vaguely suggests that he was raised, perhaps even trained, by a woman connected with one of those who concern us, perhaps employed in domestic service by one of those who concern us; more particularly, perhaps the company founded and run by the heroine financier employed her to clean its offices at night. Perhaps she brought her talented pooch with her so as to rehearse him in his stunts in such ample spaces as the lobby or the conference rooms. Such a fact would explain the dog's handiness with vacuum cleaners. He was generally known to the people of Elmira as Hoover, a name they much preferred to his baptismal Cha-cha-cha.

A photograph that was once in my possession leads me to think that the preceding series of *perhaps*'s may prove irrelevant. The photograph depicts a salon furnished in a way that makes us think "early Thirties" and "California" but *not* Hollywood. A twinkling bead curtain extends across much of the foreground. In the space to its left, underneath a faded portrait of President Hoover, a dog who is almost certainly not Cha-cha-cha but may (so great is the resemblance) well be his mother or grandmother is directing his attention to what is occurring beyond the strung beads. Just what is occurring is blurred and streaked by the front-lit strands, but surely this is Cecilia (or can it be Cecilia's mother?) standing close to a man with slick black hair and waxed moustache, to whom she is counting out a sheaf of banknotes. His head is tilted slightly forward over his outstretched hand at an angle that suggests both attentiveness and acknowledgment. And did you know that Cecilia's mother sang in a circus and at one time performed duets with a singing bitch? They don't talk much about it now that the family has risen in the world. I don't have to go into it: you will have already seen that it was via Cecilia that the dog came to be performing on that corner in upstate New York, after the romance fell through.

I first saw this photograph years ago in a pawn shop on Third Avenue, through a begrimed window, half hidden among brass objects it is hard to imagine anyone buying or even making, keyboard covers, apple sealers, snuff syringes. In these unhelpful conditions I misread it as a mildly pornographic image, with the black-haired man paying money to a naked woman — the dress worn by Cecilia or her mother was tight fitting and skin-pale. When I realized my mistake, I bought the picture, which as you know now belongs to a distinguished London dealer (none other, although he will never admit it, than the Paraguayan who inspired Ms. Taylor's succesful and unhappy partnership). This of course is where you come in, to my disgust. Your few years and positively snakelike purity have sucked more than one human into a confusion that you no doubt share while at the same time benefiting from it. And so all the elaborately and carefully reconstructed history will soon be dumped on the slop heap, even the passing movie star and little Hoover, because at bottom you revile the living, and your outspoken attraction to passionate women leads to nothing but vomiting and death — not too strong a word when one remembers your severed girl, your "sane Ophelia." But the other one you lost, the one you lost beyond recall, will never be forgotten by you, no matter what fugitive detours you may take or what pitfalls you may cleverly avoid, in the random movie-going that you day by day so assiduously cultivate, and that you call your life.

THE CHARIOT

for Niki de Saint Phalle

Wouldn't you rather go mushroom hunting? In the burnished October sky, trumpets of autumn herald the end of another year; amidst the litter of ash and birch, horns of plenty can nourish your solitary ramblings, while you delegate troubles to the experts. Think how pleasantly your sleep will come, home and warm. You'll listen to some distinguished music as you toss garlic and parsley in a lightly oiled pan; later you'll read the papers to feel abreast of things.

In the papers you read about yourself. There's no getting away from it — they've even spelled your name right, and there are only two typos: *h* and *n*, hardly sufficient excuse for you to growl with disappointment and go upstairs to soak your feet moonily in a basin of steaming water. It isn't that they've got it right — how can "they" ever get it right? — but they're waiting for more.

There they are, standing awed and respectful on the far side of a smoothly carpeted reception room. You hold an upturned trump in your left hand, and when you decide to turn it up, you can tell them modest, recognizable things. You can compare yourself to a medieval craftsman in Rheims, sculpting the smooth stone twist of a lofty rope molding, or a monk inscribing bright lizards among black words in a ponderous breviary, individual work made glorious in the collective idea of a cathedral.

You now uncover the card hidden in your left yellow sleeve: the joker. They all laugh.

You are relieved to hear them laugh. Your feet feel ridiculous in these glossy boots. You'd thought the boots would help you stride through the public halls with assurance, this way and that, but they seem to have been made of magnetized steel, and you're not even sure you're not pretending to know where the magnets are, and even that you chose to put them there. If there were just one magnet! If only someone were pointing out the way — but that's what they're expecting you to do.

You manage. The pleasant or ominous tangles of desires and feelings are as remote from you now as if you were a dancer in mid leap, sheathed in gold and silver light, mastering height and breadth and in so doing inspiring nothing if not desires and feelings among all the breathless onlookers; as if you were a fisherman who has cast his tremulous line across the surface of a pool and whose wrist stiffens against the strike, the trout stricken with hunger and pain; as if you were a judge accurately pronouncing sentence, conscious particularly of the lowered eyes of the indicted man stonily sealing up his yearning, anger, and dread as you declare what his life will now become. You manage. And you will.

You also manage their questions, because you have been designated the respondent. One of them asks you, "What is a tree?" and you answer, "A tree is a question the ground asks of the sky, and if you stay still and observe it, you will see that this is so," and all write these words down.

You would prefer having more time when you are confronted

by such problems. As you look at the others, you briefly long for a three-dimensional computer in which you could trace the entire aggregate of factors in any challenging situation, including this one. As they look at you, you see that they have found just such a complete computer, and that it is you. You cannot step out of that look, that "regard," and since this is after all one thing you have for years been striving for, in a sense you do not wish to. In any case, you have no choice — perhaps this is why you feel that you have been turned to steel and stone.

You know better, however, than to yield to such feelings. Above you, above the ceiling, above the station roof, above the delectable veil of the autumn sky, you sense the stars glittering in their unstonelike blaze, cast over the earth and its neighboring satellites like spun-silver mosquito netting. One bright star shines more powerfully than all but one of the rest — a reminder (with its legend of entrails embalmed) of mortality, and a reminder also of your lifelong, incessant, and indeed implacable journeying. That star tells you, Steer, keep steering, compel your craft and crew past the horizon into the unknown that is your first and final home. Above you, day in and day out, the twelve-spoked wheels of heaven will faithfully turn — something you can't see or feel, something that simply happens.

Sometimes you find yourself weak and repulsive. Sometimes you doubt your own eyes and ears: you watch a red cat eat the tires off your car; little yellow-testicled monkeys sit on your chest and "tell it like it is." You still hold the trump. It can be a joker again if you want, and you can still call it the seven of diamonds and let cat and monkey go their ways.

You let them go by, the good times and bum times. Today's golden afternoon, which you're glad you didn't miss, has left a pleasant glow on your skin as it disappears behind the other horizon. You go out, taking your umbrella with you, not to be on the safe side but because it provides you with a mute yet eloquent companion: its handle is carved into the head of an Indian chief smiling as he looks towards some point farther than any you can imagine.

You smile, too, as you leave to meet someone waiting for you, someone who will wait for you as long as you allow.

You have mastered the art of recognition — what to know, what cannot be known. (You recognize as well that there are things you cannot know you do not know.) You remember names. While you are not at a loss for words, you welcome the words of others. An acquaintance tells you to invest your money in Dutch real estate; another, that the Dutch property market will soon collapse. You accept their information contentedly; you draw no conclusions, make no decision.

Acceptance. One of your friends, one of your favorite friends, is a call girl. In her dizzy way she has made a success of her career — she could retire now at thirty if she felt like it, which she doesn't. She is notorious for (a) her bedroom slippers, great balls of foot-long monkey fur dyed red and blue, which she never takes off, and (b) her bed, which is set on a foundation of casters, perfectly engineered and oiled, so that in the act of lovemaking it careers unpredictably around her smooth-floored room like a lost kite in a tornado. The tickling of the fur slippers and the conniptions of the bed invariably produce — somehow without diminishing their erotic excitement — a delicious case of the giggles in every one of her customers, and often in Norma Jean herself. It helps you to think of her when you are embroiled in difficult and usually less diverting circumstances: her memory is a talisman against distress and despair.

Another memory, more distant and by now shrouded in yet other memories (smoke beaten down from towering chimneys by wind and rain; a white cart horse destroyed under the Third Avenue el): your grandfather, Ian. You came to his knees crying. He held out his right hand and said that it held one cause of your tears, his left hand another, he clapped his hands together and asked you to imagine what both hands now held (you learned to name a way out, a way ahead), and then you could climb onto his lap, from where you surveyed the world as its master, grasping your candy cane and singing the song from *The Three Little Pigs*.

You have no Ian now, or perhaps you have become your own Ian, naming the world that lies before you with assurance but without illusion, holding yourself easily straight as a dancer, like a dancer knowing that your performance of mastery is only a mastery of performance — Tweedledum and Tweedledee, no more than a snoring king's dream! — knowing that you can never reach your destination and say, Now I rule. Still, you stand handsomely on the crown of this eminence, overlooking the blond fields of harvested wheat through which your journeying has led you. You see that you did not arrive here alone, and that in this the world has served you.

At your feet a glittering, sluggish river meanders, its barge traffic freighted with gravel and coal. Eight beeches surrounding you, turned golden by the first frosts, open behind you the gloom-laden path down which you will soon start on your way. Beyond the river lies the city, laid out like a six-pointed star, the three great roads that lead to and from it stretching west, south, and north. Halfway down the slope of the hill, a man, someone who knows how to look after things, turns and waves to you with a smile.

You sit down in almost sleepy comfort to enjoy this view of the scenes of your progress. A thin mist is rising at the edges of the city, from which the sounds of daytime business are giving way to the impatient horns of late afternoon. From a suburban cafe the tune of an old favorite is brought to you on the breeze. You could, you know, go back down into that city and be welcomed as more than a departed child: as one whose very desires are objects of desire. You smile with pleasure at the prospect; with pleasure but not much curiosity.

You watch two cars follow each other out of the suburbs onto a country lane. At a three-way fork one car turns left, the other right, both cars stop, the drivers get out and converse in visible disagreement. Each had been sure; perhaps neither knew the way. They'll figure it out and get to wherever they're going. As for you, you know the way, and not where you're going. This is the gift your assurance will bring you: to be no longer sure, foreseeing only that anything can change, that everything must change, that the red sun will blacken with snow, the blue sky whiten with stars.

FRANZ KAFKA IN RIGA

The bastions of Riga enclose the old town in an irregular five-sided polygon, at each of whose corners a great tower stands, barely higher than the rest of the fortifications but projecting its mass a notable distance beyond their perimeter. Near the top of each tower lies a square platform surrounded by crenelated walls rising more than twenty feet above it. A flight of steps leads from the platform to an observation post set level with the crenelations in the outermost corner of the tower.

In the course of my tour of the northwestern tower, I decided to climb these steps in order to enjoy the view to which I imagined they would bring me. On the day of my visit this proved a difficult undertaking. Still wet from a recent shower, the steps were not only narrow but slippery, made as they were of a calcareous stone five centuries in use and worn perfectly smooth. There was no railing: after I had progressed less than half my way, I found myself obliged, in order to stay balanced, to bend over and lean one hand on the third or fourth step in front of me while with my other I groped for restraining fissures in the rough-hewn wall at my side. Even this effective if undignified tactic soon had to be abandoned when gusts of wind from above threatened to blow away my cap. I finished my ascent more or less on my hands and knees, or rather my *hand* and knees, with my other hand clapped on top of my head — a posture that provoked derisive laughter from my companions below, although I scarcely heard them through the shudders of dizziness that had by now begun to afflict me. When at last I reached the vantage point so laboriously striven for, I beheld, instead of Riga and the waters of the Baltic, only unbroken fog, as dingy as an old newspaper under the clouded sky.

Several weeks later, when I was back home, a friend who knew I had gone to Riga showed me a passage in Kafka's notebooks describing his sojourn there. One paragraph read:

"I decided to climb these steps in order to enjoy the view to which they would bring me. On the day of my visit this proved a difficult undertaking. Still wet from a recent shower, the steps were not only narrow but slippery, made as they were of a calcareous stone five centuries in use and worn perfectly smooth. There was no railing: after I had progressed less than half my way, I found myself obliged, in order to stay balanced, to bend over and lean one hand on the third or fourth step in front of me while with my other I groped for restraining fissures in the rough-hewn wall at my side. Even this effective if undignified tactic soon had to be abandoned when gusts of wind from above threatened to blow away my hat. I finished my ascent more or less on my hands and knees, or rather my *hand* and knees, with my other hand clapped on top of my head — a posture that provoked derisive laughter from my companions below, although I scarcely heard them through the shudders of dizziness that had by now begun to afflict me. When at last I reached the vantage point so laboriously strived for, I beheld, instead of Riga and the waters of the

Baltic, only unbroken fog, as dingy as an old newspaper under the clouded sky."

I was angry that Kafka had rendered this experience with such unaccountable inaccuracy. In saying this, I am not referring to his hat, which had nothing to do with my feelings; or, at least, nothing particular.

STILL LIFE

Left is where you start: an iron door fitted with small glass panes; beside it, seen through a bay window, a terrace garden, with leafless trees and shrubs, among them a gingko; beyond, in the middle of a tidal river, which the terrace hides, a ruined island interrupting a view of the far shore. To the right of the garden a brick wall, checkered with rectangular windows, its top too high to be visible, closes the space outside. Although it is almost noon, the wall is in shadow.

Facing you, a shut white door; next to it, a narrow floor-to-ceiling bookcase filled with books, most of them about your paternal forebears or your father's business, which was architecture. Beyond, another door, then an architect's worktable (this is your dead father's office), long, flat, and deep, equipped with large square drawers or wide shallow ones. The far end of the room is concealed by a partition, against which are set a filing cabinet and a small metal desk with an electric typewriter on it. Along the wall that runs behind you at right angles to the partition, there is a commodious sofa upholstered in rough beige material, with a low table in front of it — a square of thick plate glass on an X-shaped chromed steel base.

You sit at a desk whose off-white expanse is finished in some composite substance, matt but smooth. Small objects lie along the edges of the desk — pencils, pens, erasers, scissors, cigars, a paper cutter, a magnifying glass. Three blank pages are spread out on the surface in front of you. The first is a bare patch of earth that you must ingeniously impregnate with apparently exhausted seed; your consolation is supposed to lie in calling it your own. The second — more like a draftsman's sheet: punctiliousness and alertness are in order — is for rendering what someone else has already depicted in other words; a hard but useful job. The third page is a false page: in fact it is a staging area for words that are destined for speech, and a rough diagram of the Alice's mirror through which they will be spoken: the mirror in which, when you look at yourself, it is others that you see.

The air in the room is warm, bright with the morning light. The faded taste in your mouth is of tobacco and *café au lait.*

There are some words now on each of the three pages. You get up and go out.

The next room is lofty and windowless — no, there is a small window recessed high in one corner: its light is absorbed in the bluish glow cast by six long fluorescent ceiling tubes. The walls and ceiling of the room are white, the floor and cupboards gray, the fuse box and wall telephone black. Its long narrow space gives an impression of smoothness — surfaces merge in the diffused light, continuity is punctuated rather than broken by the glitter of artifacts (glasses, a chromed kettle, a bottle of red wine). The only books here are a short shelf of cookbooks, the only pages to be written on those of a little pad for listing errands, with a blunt stubby pencil alongside it.

There is a smell of breaded meat cooking in butter. White wine is washing from your teeth the taste of coffee and cigar.

A woman is standing at the far end of the kitchen. The knuckles of her hand are swollen. She holds herself very erect. Her hair, of medium length, is dyed light brown and has been carefully brushed so as to rise above her face like a coronet. Her pale, faintly mottled skin is smooth across her cheeks and forehead, wrinkled under her chin. Her eyes are shadowed and her lips reddened; she seems about to smile or speak. She is wearing a cotton smock over a patterned dress of thin blue wool.

You stand in front of the wall telephone. This woman has given you a message: you are to call a number in the city. You have done this, and you are listening in the receiver to another woman's voice. It is making an announcement for which you are unprepared, although it is not altogether surprising. It is its effect on you that is surprising. The announcement is of an arrival — her arrival.

The effect, which you think may be due to the imminency, almost the immediateness of this arrival, is to remove time from your grasp. Through the morning, through preceding days and even weeks, you had allowed expectations about this predictable day to lay down in your mind their rows of comforting waysigns. These have now vanished. The hours ahead have been condemned to uncertainty, you now know that the hours behind were saturated with illusion. Time has lost its havens. You feel as though you had come, after a long drive, to a house you had driven to countless times before, walked up to the second overturned flowerpot from the right, and found no key.

Through the window, you see the terrace garden with its gingko tree overlooking the invisible river. Above the ruined island the sky is clearing. The wall of bricks and windows is darker because of the brighter sky, and because the sun is in the south and declining.

No longer completely shut, the white door faces you beside the bookcase and its books about your father's family and profession. You wonder if it would be easier working standing up at the worktable, or typing at the electric typewriter. You would like to lie down on the sofa and read.

There must be a smell of fresh cigar smoke in the warm air (your head is too full of smoke to tell).

No new words have appeared on any of the three pages in front of you. Your attention is like a dog restlessly waiting for a master. You lie down on the sofa to read and wait.

Through the window, all that can be seen is the wall of bricks and glass, and the gingko tree standing against the bright blue afternoon sky. The door facing the desk has been opened; the door to the right of the bookcase is now ajar. The architect's worktable and the partition are no longer in view. On the desk chair, on the chair belonging to the smaller desk, on the knobs of the doors, articles of clothing are strewn and hung: perhaps two ring-neck sweaters (one yellow, one rust), dark-blue stretch jeans stitched with white, a light-blue cotton shirt, tan flannel slacks; or gray slacks, a belted brown wool skirt, a turtleneck sweater; or a khaki pelisse and a navy-blue cardigan with four brass buttons. Other clothing may lie out of sight on the floor, where, nevertheless, a pair of cherry-red high-heeled boots can be seen, one upright, the other tipped onto its side.

Taste: another one. Sensations: the other you. (Whether mouth or crypt.) You have come back from what seems — but this is mistaken — like a distance. Years ago, when you first appeared, you were hard to hold, and now are the one that holds. Your rediscovery has come almost too harshly, in these first moments — a present of roses ripped open with both hands for their rosecolor and scent, in a smarting forgetfulness of thorns.

Sleep comes next. After sleep, through a fringe of hair, the wall and the slanting gingko are almost featureless against the midafternoon sky, blue with a glow of gold. The light in the room is darker. The two white doors are mauve-gray. Clothes on furniture and floor are pleated with dark. Only a threadlike gleam shines from the tubing of the desk chair.

Taste: you. Smell: you. Sensations: you, and sofa upholstery — rough, hot. (Whether mouth or earth.) The tale you have to tell is wordless, even if words rush after you to fill what is anything but a void — at least no more a void than before. It is like being inside a comfortable house (one, perhaps, with four overturned flowerpots on the stoop), opening a door at night on a familiar view: there is nothing familiar in the moonstruck world outside.

Sleep comes next. After sleep, the sky has paled above the rim of a shoulder. The wall, the gingko tree, the tubular chair, and the shirt hanging from the chair are all solid black. The gold in the sky has deepened to green bronze. Books on shelves are dim stripes of brown and black. The floor is awash in shadow.

Sleep came next. It was like swimming in a warm sea, off a coast of sand and rock, plunging repeatedly beneath the surface and staying under as long as breath would allow to relish the dispersed sunlight, the blurred outcroppings, the glint of fish, emerging to gulp air and blink with salt and brightness, plunging again. . . . At one point the shore is out of sight.

Many shadows in the brick wall — some curtained, some not — were lighting up. By now the sky beyond the window was dark, except for the glow rising in front of it from the city's lights, although his emanation changed the sky less than a red speck of plane distantly traversing it. The sky was altogether dark, with the close-in darkness of late midwinter afternoons, filled with the swell of homebound traffic. There was little to see, less to say, before a last brief sleep, taken in the knowledge that when I awoke she would no longer be there, and that she would never leave me.

III

Calibrations of Latitude

DEAR MOTHER

for James Tate and in memory of William Cullen Bryant

This is where I once saw a deaf girl playing in a field. Because I did not know how to approach her without startling her, or how I would explain my presence, I hid. I felt so disgusting, I might as well have raped the child, a grown man on his belly in a field watching a deaf girl play. My suit was stained by the grass and I was an hour late for dinner. I was forced to discard my suit for lack of a reasonable explanation to my wife, a hundred dollar suit! We're not rich people, not at all. So there I was, left to my wool suit in the heat of summer, soaked through by noon each day. I was an embarrassment to the entire firm: it is not good for the morale of the fellow worker to flaunt one's poverty. After several weeks of crippling tension, my superior finally called me into his office. Rather than humiliate myself by telling him the truth, I told him I would wear whatever damned suit I pleased, a suit of armor if I fancied. It was the first time I had challenged his authority. And it was the last. I was dismissed. Given my pay. On the way home I thought, I'll tell her the truth, yes, why not! Tell her the simple truth, she'll love me for it. What a touching story. Well, I didn't. I don't know what happened, a loss of courage, I suppose. I told her a mistake I had made had cost the company several thousand dollars, and that not only was I dismissed, I would also somehow have to find the money to repay them the sum of my error. She wept, she beat me, she accused me of everything from malice to impotency. I helped her pack and drove her to the bus station. It was too late to explain. She would never believe me now. How cold the house was without her. How silent. Each plate I dropped was like tearing the flesh from a living animal. When all were shattered, I knelt in a corner and tried to imagine what I would say to her, the girl in the field. What did it matter what I said, since she wouldn't hear me? I could say anything I liked.

Next day after eating lunch out of a plastic container I went back to the field. I'd found my stained suit on the floor of the closet where I'd dumped it. The added rumpling and dirt made it look even worse. I put it on anyway — I'd been wearing it at the beginning of this misadventure, and I wanted to be wearing it at the end. I do not know if this was a mistake or not. The little girl was playing not far from where I'd seen her the first time. I stood at some distance inside the edge of the field and spoke to her in a voice neither loud nor soft. I said that my wife's lawyer had called earlier to say that she was filing for divorce, but that I would never blame her, the little girl, for that. I told her that she was beautiful, that in a way I loved her, that even though I was utterly unhappy I would remember the scene of her in the field without bitterness. I had more to say, but the girl had stood up and turned to me as though she had heard me, which it soon transpired she had. She was not so little, either, but rather tall and, as she approached me, plainly of a more nubile constitution than I had conceived from afar. She pointed toward me and in a confident voice cried, "That's him!" to persons that were out of my sight for the good reason that they were standing behind me, three men and two women in serious garb, whom I took to be officials of some sort. I then sank into such torment that I suffered a kind of seizure, from whose effects I have taken several months to recover. It turned out that I could not have fallen into better hands, for those five strangers were medical people, and they have tended me, I assure you, with extraordinary care. My indisposition nevertheless has kept me from writing to you sooner, and that is why now, before recounting the most recent events, dear Mother, I hasten to send you the melancholy intelligence of what has recently happened to me.

Early on the evening of the eleventh day of the present month I was at a neighboring house in this village. Several people of both sexes were assembled in one of the apartments, and three or four others, with myself, were in another. At last came in a little elderly gentleman, pale, thin, with a solemn countenance, hooked nose, and hollow eyes. It was not long before we were summoned to attend in the apartment where he and the rest of the company were gathered. We went in and took our seats; the little elderly gentleman with the hooked nose prayed, and we all stood up. When he had finished, most of us sat down. The gentleman with the hooked nose then muttered certain cabalistical expressions which I was much too frightened to remember, but I recollect that at the conclusion I was given to understand that I was married to a young lady of the name of Juniper Simmons, whom I perceived standing by my side, and I hope in the course of a few months to have the pleasure of introducing to you as your daughter-in-law, which is a matter of some interest to the poor girl, who has neither father nor mother in the world.

I looked only for goodness of heart, an ingenuous and affectionate disposition, a good understanding, etc., and the character of my wife is too frank and single-hearted to suffer me to fear that I may be disappointed. I do myself wrong; I did not look for these nor any other qualities, but they trapped me before I was aware, and now I am married in spite of myself.

Thus the current of destiny carries us along. None but a madman would swim against the stream, and none but a fool would exert himself to swim with it. The best way is to float quietly with the tide.

MR. SMATHERS

Late in the summer of my eleventh year, I decided to butcher our neighbors' Afghan hound. One afternoon I went out to stalk him as he prowled around backyards, hoping to lure him with a red plastic bowl full of sugared water that had been laced with poison. I caught up with him just when he'd soiled our very own cosmos patch, an event that was actually a bright spot in the proceedings because it justified them. He wasn't a mean dog, or a bright dog, just a soiler. Hence my longing to butcher him. There was another reason. He not only soiled sidewalks and gardens: he embarrassed me again and again with his great stalk of a penis. It was as though he waited till I was near him to start making water, he would lift his leg and brandish his dong as if it were some kind of lure, a lure meant for me, when it was anything but a lure, it made me blush and squirm and yearn to dissolve in the bright summer haze.

I was standing there, after setting down the bowl of water in the dog's general vicinity, when the butcher, who was passing by, stopped and looked at me. He had a stalk of alfalfa in his teeth, a stalk quivering green against the red and white of his soiled smock. I suddenly felt hungry looking at that smock soiled with the blood of pigs and beeves, something that I knew shouldn't normally lure a boy like me. The butcher, chewing on his stalk, asked me what I was doing. "You don't look exactly bright standing there like some kind of drooping asshole."

I turned to the butcher and indicated the nosing dog, now approaching the red bowl of water. I said, "You got any idea what's in that bowl of water? Sugar and rat poison."

The butcher glanced around. Did he notice our soiled flower bed? In any case, when I asked him, "By the way, how do you butcher a big dog like him?," it was as though a lure of spellbinding fascination had risen before the butcher's eyes. His gaze grew almost frighteningly bright, his mouth opened and the spittle-spotted stalk of alfalfa started sliding down his smock. I pointed this out to him. "The stalk—"

"Fuck the stalk, sonny. First thing we gotta do is get rid of that water. No way to eat the fella if his meat's all soiled with rat stuff. I'll go fetch a nice bone, we'll lure him over with that, I'll get an icepick to fix his brain, then we can butcher him together. I'm no slouch as a dog-butcher, believe me. I've stalked dachshunds in Central Park in my time. With a turd for lure."

I started making water in my pants. Even my socks were soiled. I'd never guessed the butcher was so bright.

BRENDAN

Whatever happened to me the first time I saw his face in a crowd? I'm not attracted to men, I certainly wasn't charmed by the oil in his hair, and his general appearance (bearing, etc.) suggested a ruin rather than someone of monumental interest. But his pinched lips made me think of the oboe, my favorite instrument; and, as it turned out, his very own.

I had nothing at stake in approaching him, which I did as casually as I could, my interest deepening the more we spoke. And it wasn't only my interest but a strange affection that began deepening, as unsuspected — or at least not rationally predictable — qualities illuminated his face through its wrinkles, blotches, and warts.

One look he gave me drove a stake through my usually sceptical heart, and I felt as though I'd struck oil in a desert or, more aptly, come upon an oasis. He had been speaking about playing the oboe and its difficulties: the nightmare of uncertain reeds, how the pressure can ruin the brain (the pressure of breath painstakingly retained) — a ruin not immediately threatening him but always potentially there and only deepening with time. And yet, he said, he would rather lose his wits than give up the oboe. As he spoke he turned

towards me and looked straight into my face with a gaze part suppli-
cation, part defiance. Then he grinned and asked me to pass the olive
oil.

We were by now seated in a bar-and-grill he knew, The Silver
Stake, and had been enjoying the house cocktail, a dry martini called
the Silver Stake Stinker. It featured a slice of garlic in place of the
customary olive, which you'd think might ruin the drink but didn't:
it simply floated an imperceptibly thin layer of oil of garlic on top of it
which, together with the touch of vermouth, succeeded in deepening the fragrance of the gin without calling attention to itself, an
effect that on the face of it was as inexplicable as it was real.

My new friend who played the oboe was named Brendan
Gillespie, born in a village in County Clare where no one had even
heard of an oboe. But neighbors had a gramophone; and one rainy
summer afternoon, past the full-uddered black-and-white goat teth-
ered to a stake in the front yard, he entered that house and within
the hour came face to face with his destiny: "Jesu, Joy of Man's De-
siring," with oboe obbligato. Then and there, to the ruin of his modest expectations, he too became "obliged," the haunting reedy ec-
stacy only deepening through distressed nights and distracted days, a
fervent itch no herbal salve or maternal oil could soothe.

He walked to Dublin. He took an unpopular job as scuffer in an
oil cannery, sleeping in a storeroom. He saved enough to rent and at
last buy an oboe. He won the sympathy of a teacher, taking lessons,
learning fast, his passion deepening with his skill. He could read music
before he read words. He knew his whole being was at stake. And
times were hard. He emigrated to America in steerage. For weeks he
hovered on the brink of utter ruin, finally landing his first job in the
Poughkeepsie Pops. After that he was able to face the music.

Later, at his place, face to face, I watched Brendan oil his keys. Then he played Groff's "Oboe Ruin," Ruiz's "Lament at the Stake," and eventually "Jesu, Joy . . ." as the night kept deepening.

THE BROADCAST

The problem with many of our lives is that they're so often routine: we're busy with this and that, and then in our free time we just doodle inconsequentialities. But last night I happened to listen to a radio broadcast that explained how you could put everything you needed in life into one sock. I don't know why, but this suddenly brought me to life like the sound of a trumpet. I know the concept was lunatic, I know I'd be hard put to describe why I was tickled, thrilled, and convinced all at once. Let *me* describe as best as I can what this man told us.

You carefully check your daily routine and notice what you use out of habit and not need — obviously the angel-trumpet blossoms in your backyard that you stop and look at so fondly, or the doodle-bugs that you approve of chasing ants at their roots do not belong in that sock, neither does (any more) the newspaper where you read about the broadcast in the first place.

(You did check it to see if there were plans to repeat the broadcast since you hadn't recorded it and there were things that I found difficult to describe to myself after it was over – perhaps I could write the station about the sock program's availability, for them things like that must be pretty routine, all those guys and their secretaries sitting around with nothing to do but doodle on their memo pads and pass each other notes, like "You really need an ear-trumpet, you've asked me to repeat myself the last three times we spoke, even though I trumpet what I say loud and clear," obviously it's not the office staff that created that broadcast, some genius, my God I've already forgotten his name, no it was Preston Doodle, although I can't remember if he wrote it or was just there to describe the project, I don't think so though, his voice wasn't pro, more like routine, with just that touch of weirdness that would think of putting your life in a sock.)

It has just occurred to me that what I heard as "into one sock" was actually "into one stock." Maybe I'm the one who needs an ear-trumpet.

Jesus that would mean that everything that electrified me was only routine advice and I was a victim of my own wish fulfillment listening to that broadcast. I'm afraid that at this moment my feelings are becoming too painful to describe, it's as though a cruel God had taken a Q-tip and started to doodle inside my ear, inside my brain, inside my soul, the doodle of despair which I guess is all my life is worth — not worth sticking in a sock even. Still, maybe I can do something with the idea, maybe describe it to some friends as if it were a game we could play. Or I could take up the trumpet and get to be so hot on it I'd end up making records and get broadcast myself, yeah, why not.

Meanwhile, it's not so bad in here, sometimes the routine gets screwed up -- I mean my own routine. The supervisors all doodle. The janitor watches one TV broadcast after another. I look at my sock and pretend it's a golden trumpet too glorious to describe.

CALIBRATIONS OF LATITUDE

I

On a sunny Wednesday morning in early May, rigorous of mind and sound of body in spite of advancing years, Sir Joseph Pernican set forth on his quest. He felt, in addition to confidence, a provocative unease. The familiar man who had provided his instructions had signified that the clues he would find on his way would take unexpected guises; divining them would depend on his accepting them attentively and without prejudice. Sir Joseph was sure at least of his starting-point. He had also chosen what impressed him as the most likely (because most eastwards) path. But although he had been informed of the principles that must guide him, he had no certainty as to how those principles should be applied, nor did he know what he was meant to find, except for this: its discovery would provide an explanation, and a definitive one.

As he stepped onto the sidewalk, he turned to the right, thereafter crossing several streets on the way to his first stopping place: a street that once led to a sand pit; a street commemorating yet another Napoleonic general; a market street that despite change still retained an old-fashioned image of its earlier self; bordering a cemetery, a street renamed for a heroic fireman.

He entered a large circular square, which he partially skirted. A crowd of people some distance away was packing itself into a subway entrance. He left behind a temple-like building, whose one remaining function was to serve as gateway to a domain hidden beneath him, a world of cloudy hewed chalk. He did not bother to consider, at the center of the square, a shrunk bronze beast.

Sir Joseph arrived at his first transitional destination: a modern six-story building close to the junction of two narrowly intersecting avenues. It housed offices of the national airline. He wondered whether he had not miscalculated his distance, reassuring himself with the observation that the arc of the square's perimeter he had traversed was equal to about one third of its circumference. He repressed a slight regret at not having headed somewhat more to the left (to the north). He entered the airline's passenger agency but noticed nothing remarkable. He approached the information counter, where a very old man stood listening to a young blonde hostess. Standing behind him, Sir Joseph saw that a large, detailed map had been spread out on the glass-topped surface. Completely unfolded, the map would have represented the entire globe, with Italy placed at its center. In the middle of Italy was portrayed the figure of a Roman hero dressed in helmet, breastplate, skirt, and greaves, carrying a short broad-bladed sword, identified by a scroll as Aeneas.

The airline attendant was pointing out either itineraries or distances between northeastern Italian towns; she had drawn freehand lines between Vicenza and Udine as well as between Udine and Venice. The old man uttered no word in response to her remarks, only an occasional thin wheeze. When she had apparently finished, he abruptly drew a pistol from his pocket and began waving it towards France and southern Germany. Dreading the consequences not only to the young woman but to his inquiry, Sir Joseph at once requested she pay no further attention to her interlocutor and speak to him instead. The woman looked at him in astonishment. Sir Joseph then saw that what the old man held in his hand was not a pistol but a combined compass and protractor, a sight that encouraged him greatly: in his circumstances, the instrument made perfect sense.

He left the agency forthwith, superstitiously going round twice through the revolving door. He decided that the lines inscribed by the attendant on the map confirmed his general, if not exact, choice of direction. But where, he asked himself, might he find a sign of the complement of the space in which and beyond which he had been instructed to proceed? And what was the coefficient of multiplication?

Emerging, he turned left around the sharp corner into the neighboring avenue, just in time to overtake a pair of slower-moving students, one of whom was saying to the other, "And here we enter a neighborhood of hospitals and focal jails."

II

Staying on the left-hand sidewalk for no reason except that it paralleled his thoughts, he made his way down the avenue once known as the "lower way," past the lost château at the extremity of things, along the street of astronomers, stopping only briefly at the Hôtel de l'Europe, where he had once stayed as a young man. Through its glass entrance door sunlight penetrated the dark interior. He stepped inside: the painting had not budged. How could they still take such risks? He summarily refreshed his memory of Millet's "Peasant's Tomb," a farm landscape with an eloquent stub of a stake marking the burial place of the title. Sir Joseph hastened on. He came to another wide thoroughfare, it too once a Roman road. His progress was halted by a crowd of tourists waiting outside a gate that opened onto the grounds of a handsome eighteenth-century mansion. He had decided to cross the street to avoid the gathering when, reviewing his notes, he learned that he had reached his second stop. He waited: soon a guardian appeared and opened the gate, not allowing the visitors to pass, however, until he had delivered a few introductory remarks. Those entering, he said, were aware that the main object of their visit was the collection of embossed silver exhibited in the house. He nevertheless recommended their taking particular notice on their way in of another, less reputed attraction: an early nineteenth-century anthill, whose conservation had been a condition laid down by the last hereditary owner for the bequest of his property to the state. The administration had accepted the stipulation, provided one of their own was respected: the donor must protect the neighborhood from a proliferation of ants by maintaining a ring of seventeen doodlebugs around the base of the anthill, whose inhabitants would have their nourishment guaranteed by their public owners. These provisions were readily agreed upon.

After the guardian and his flock had disappeared amid the abundant greenery of the park, Sir Joseph pursued his way. He believed he had understood the lesson of what he had just witnessed: he must confine himself to the zone of his undertaking and abandon all regret in regard to possibilities not chosen. But where was the promised reflection of that zone to be found? He imagined an inverted cone penetrating the earth underneath the anthill's settled hump.

.

III

Sir Joseph crossed a boulevard thronged with faces of protest and thought of the fields of vine, garden, sainfoin, and lucerne grass that had once stretched beyond it. He passed close behind the great church but avoided entering it, out of fear of its legendary "spirit pumps," which reputedly still worked their unnerving effect on visitors, of whom, he noticed, many were pushing their way inside through a lateral door. Did they, any better than he, understand the motto of the monks whose domain this once was: "Those who water heaven will hate its fruits"? Why did these words frighten him? Did a spirit pump empty the believer of the "water" which he might use to irrigate the heavenly fields? He shivered inwardly in childish shame at his bodily fluids, urine and seed. Didn't he hope, so late in his life, to reap whatever fruits awaited him once he reached his goal?

In the meantime, his next goal proved disappointing: nothing was there. He could only perceive unmanifest relics of the past, from which the female deaf-mutes and beneficiaries of evangelical charity had long since vanished. Might Miss MacDonald still be found in the office of the Buddhist grammarian? It lay outside his path; he recalled the lesson of the anthill. One small street displayed a house bridging its entrance, with a grating (now open) underneath. The street was empty, its façades were devoid of meaning to him. He again walked round the intersection.

In the nearest café Sir Joseph ordered a coffee with hot milk. The barman was polite and indifferent. A couple standing next to him began arguing about a recent development in the neighborhood. Sir Joseph could not grasp what it was and requested they explain. Both man and woman then began recounting their versions simultaneously. Sir Joseph succeeded in deciphering these facts: a new breed of cockroaches had appeared in certain adjacent streets; the cockroaches left trails of slime that, when they came into contact with any inorganic chemical (like those in all insecticides), ignited with a low-intensity, long-burning flame; thus far damage had been minor, but clearly a huge potential danger existed. The woman claimed to have witnessed the phenomenon in action, the man insisted it must have been due to other causes, such as the coincidental proximity of cockroaches and particularly inflammable substances. The barman declined to take sides in the discussion. Sir Joseph thanked them for the information before leaving.

On the sidewalk a scruffy man handed him a yellow leaflet written in Portuguese. Sir Joseph perused it rapidly, then tossed the crumpled sheet in the gutter. From its thousand words he had salvaged no more than one capital C under which a cedilla had been exaggerated into the likeness of a viper.

He could make nothing of this, or of anything else. He felt disappointed, abandoned, and confused like, he thought, the blank *e* of an unaccented syllable spoken by someone else. He then saw the point. He had been given an exemplary lesson, a preparatory one, no doubt, but exemplary all the same. He had been first warned, and now convincingly taught: situations are to be accepted "without prejudice."

Sir Joseph reflected on the tools at his disposal. The ratio of two to one had evidently worked as a measure of the distance between his stations. But he still could not deduce the multiplicand on which 1.7320 must operate; nor could he any longer permit himself to speculate on the nature of that "other half" that would supply whatever was wanting from this present angulation.

IV

He came to a partly ruined chapel. Its yard was forbiddingly enclosed by a nine-foot wall whose gates were bricked up. Across one of them an inscription read:

> *The King forbids that God should do*
> *Miracles here for me and you.*

Inside the chapel he found, as he hoped, a pamphlet relating its history.

The pamphlet declared (summarizing Larrey's thesis) that the persecution of the Jansenists originated at a time long before Clement XI. Its basis was the favor shown by Pius IV to the rural constituency of the church to the detriment of its restless urban elements. It was as a result of this attitude that the Jansenists were later attacked: the cause was thus political rather than purely doctrinal. The consequences are well known: Clement XI's bull *Unigenitus*; the protests it aroused in the French church and university; the support it received from Louis XIV and Madame de Maintenon, which led to 20,000 arrests, to the systematic refusal of the sacraments to Jansenists, to the proclamation in 1730 that the bull *Unigenitus* was the law of the land. To counter such persecution, the Jansenist congregations created a secret fund known as "Perec's Box" (*la boîte à Perec*), which helped them survive this difficult period and eventually, in alliance with the Philosophers, drive the Jesuits, their chief enemies, out of France.

In 1727 a celebrated Jansenist, Pascal de Frangy, having died of self-inflicted mortifications, was buried in a common grave in the yard of the now-ruined chapel. Soon afterwards, the black marble slab placed as a memorial over the grave became a much-frequented meeting-place for his friends and admirers and, subsequently, the scene of a veritable cult. Legends sprang up about the grave, and there was much talk of miracles occurring there. An extraordinary fervor came to animate the graveyard visitors. Fits accompanied by visions were frequent; and in order to induce such propitious states, those seeking inspiration, who were mostly women, resorted to extravagant acts. They dug out the ground under the slab in order to devour it; they asked vigorous lads called "relievers" to pinch and twist their breasts and trample on their limbs. Witnesses report their being beaten with logs, meanwhile crying out, "Oh, how good this is! What good it does me! Brother, if you can endure it, I beg you not to stop!" They swallowed red-hot coals and bound bibles, had fifty-pound blocks dropped on them from a considerable height, were nailed to a cross, or had their tongues pierced.

The royal police did not intervene for several years; at last, in 1732, they built a high wall around the graveyard and sealed its entrances, which were placed under permanent guard. It was at this time that the couplet noticed by Sir Joseph was inscribed by a disappointed follower, who with his fellows was obliged to perform penances and miracles in private dwellings, where the ranks of graves became surely no more than a fading and ultimately forgotten recollection.

In a short time Sir Joseph found himself at his next destination, on a little street one block from the botanical gardens. Realizing where he was, he was filled with gloom: the place was one filled with regret for something he had never known, for a past out of his reach. He wished for a moment that he had followed another route. But, he reminded himself, what if this one was supremely right? Had he here begun to learn the nature of that missing invisible half that he had proved incapable of imagining, the empire of the dead from which he had, perhaps mistakenly, been praying for escape? Had its hand lain waiting, by no means hidden but mistily ignored, to rest itself on his shoulder at this surprising moment?

V

It was still in some despondency that Sir Joseph traversed the avenues of the botanical gardens, among towering trees, one of which was labeled with its botanical name and date of planting. He hurried through the zoo, where raucous undisciplined clusters of children ("fit for the stables," Sir Joseph thought) waited to be led in among monkeys and tigers. He came to the bank of the river. Here kings and courtesans had bathed naked centuries ago. He at once guessed it was not for such history that he was here, but for a half-forgotten memory of his own, one from his days as a young man. The memory did not concern him directly; indeed it had come back to him seemingly by chance.

Not far to his left lay a river port, one principally used in earlier years for the commerce of wine. A Chinese wood-dealer, then of an age that in most men would recommend retirement and repose, availed himself of the port for the delivery at an exceptionally low price of timber rare or seasoned: the reason being that no duty had ever been paid on it. The unloading of such contraband had necessarily to be effected as quickly and secretly as possible. It was therefore carried out in the very first glimmer of daylight by a few loyal, expert handlers. The Chinaman also relied on an ingenious method he had contrived to ensure a rapid getaway, should the need arise. During the unloadings, rather than moor his barge to the wharf, he dropped a special stern anchor ten yards aft of his barge and (depending on the strength of the current) five to twelve yards distant from the bank. It was the current itself, by pivoting the barge at a calculated angle, that then maintained it in place against the quay. In case of discovery by the fiscal police, one blow of a hammer was enough to spring the anchor-chain from its capstan as soon as the barge had swung out into the river to initiate its escape — a far swifter mode of departure than one requiring a double disengagement of ropes from bollards.

The Chinaman had never had to put his subterfuge to the test. But he never abandoned it, for a simple reason: it made him feel inordinately proud. He was equally proud of only one other thing in his life, and that was his wife. He had married her fifty years before, when she was a mere fourteen, and she had never ceased bringing him pleasure and happiness. Unfortunately he was not only proud of her but obsessively jealous, a sentiment that might have been expected to lessen as the couple aged but that on the contrary had only grown in intensity, to such an extent that he first resorted during his absences to confining her to their house, then to their bedroom, last of all imprisoning her in a contraption of his own devising, a five-foot box divided lengthwise, between whose halves she was gently but firmly enclosed from neck to ankle. It is true that the box was a marvel of comfort, lined, for instance, with velvet-covered padding, it is also true that it was only used when her husband left her for a few hours — he could not bear longer separations and would never think of taking one of his river journeys without her. But it is no less true that his wife found this treatment cruel and unbearably humiliating. When years of entreaty had brought no change, she at last fell back on a somewhat desperate expedient to put an end to it.

She one day announced to her husband that unless he dispensed with his box she would lay on him a curse preserved in her family since the Shang Dynasty. The effect of the curse would be to destroy his barge. He only laughed at her. She pronounced the curse and repeated it day after day, week after week. Not unreasonably, he became somewhat irritated and no less incredulous. The two then left together for a coastal port to pick up a consignment of teak.

During this time the wife had put their stay in the city to good use. With the collaboration of her son, sympathetic to her plight, she succeeded in taking measurements of the special anchor, in having a plaster mould of it made, and finally in having it cast in solid sugar weighted with a quantity of small lead balls. Painted a convincing rust-flecked black, the replica was smuggled aboard the barge at the last stop before the city and substituted for the original. When they had docked in the capital, having made sure her husband was safely ashore, the wife for the last time repeated her curse in ringing tones. Once again her husband fretfully shrugged off her words. She soon had the heady albeit mixed pleasure of watching their beloved barge suddenly bump against the craft moored ahead of it before gyrating out into the river, where in the first rays of the nascent day she, and he, saw it smash tremendously against a stone pier of the first bridge downstream.

The wood merchant agreed to get rid of the vicious box and end every form of confinement, provided his wife swear to never again exercise a Shang curse against him and, as well, to solemnly renew their marriage vows.

Sir Joseph readily drew a moral: without trust, he would never arrive at his goal.

Along the embankment an avenue ran east — another, more distant allusion to a definitive past.

VI

He detoured across the river over an irrelevant bridge, crossed the end of a boulevard, continued over a canal on a footway named after it, something that seemed to favor thought and progress (but had he shown himself capable of thought? could his walking be considered progress?); then, breasting two streams of cars, Sir Joseph found himself on rue Jésus-Christ. He disliked the portentousness of the name and the brevity of the street. He entered it all the same, advanced a few yards, and stopped by a red-granite monument on its right-hand sidewalk: a three-foot-high irregular solid whose smooth rounded sides sloped up to a bent tip, a tip drooping as if in dejection. An inscription running around the base had been, save for a few separate letters, clumsily chipped off, as had an ornament at its peak. Having observed Sir Joseph's bemusement, a tailor stepped from his shop to speak to him. He said that the stone had been erected here in 1869, the year when the street had been opened, its name chosen in homage to a recently published biography of Our Lord by Napoleon III. During the inauguration of the street, the Emperor had noticed a swan on the waters of the canal; dispatching an aide to the nearest bakery for a pound of stale bread, he left his entourage in the midst of the ceremony to briefly nourish the majestic fowl. During the following months Napoleon several times returned to indulge a similar fancy. At such times he would lie face down on the edge of the embankment, stretched on a thick embroidered towel laid out for this purpose by an attendant, with a crust-filled basket at his side from which he hopefully tossed morsels into the stagnant canal; no swan ever returned, except once, when a male bird flew overhead, proceeding from the river towards some unknown destination. At its sight the Emperor was heard to exclaim, "O my swan, my swan!" It seems that, notwithstanding their outcome, these excursions distracted him from the ever-increasing pain brought on by politics and calculi.

Sir Joseph thanked the tailor. Alone, he wondered if this clearly predestined information meant that he should relinquish his own calculations, such as multiplication and the comparison of angles, as well as his reflections on the possible forms of a likeness that would complete the reality he merely perceived. What might have happened to him on the other side of the canal, or one street up? Why had he begun feeling a new sort of melancholy? In terms of his exploration, were his feelings of any consequence or merely impediments to be ignored and even suppressed?

VII

Now on the fourth and last of the longer legs of his journey, he passed the obliterated site of an author's theater and crossed one street where he had once eaten *veau Marengo*, another named for a transvestite gardener, a third famous for its trolls.

Having carefully reckoned the distance he must go, Sir Joseph was surprised on his arrival to find himself in yet another little street where nothing attracted his eye or mind. As earlier, he entered the café closest by. A plump, smiling woman in late middle-age sat behind the cash register; a youth tended the bar; in front of it, five men of strikingly varied ages and dress stood affably passing round a stemmed glass containing at least a pint of clear liquid the color of cherry candy. Sir Joseph had no sooner taken a place next to them than one, a florid ill-shaven man in his forties, clad in rough, worn corduroy and laced knee-boots, tipped the oversize wine glass between his lips and emptied it. This act provoked the immediate disapproval of all and the fury of some. One man, shaking his fist in the offender's astonished face as he railed against him, looked ready to come to blows. Peace was restored by the plump cashier. She quickly refilled a second large glass while admonishing the irate customer: he should remember that the fellow was freshly arrived from Sardinia, had a limited acquaintance with their language, and had certainly failed to understand their drinking rule when it had been expounded to him.

Turning to Sir Joseph, plainly bewildered at what had taken place, the woman forthwith gave him a brief explanation. The great hospital at the center of their neighborhood bore the name of the monastery in which it had originated, whose monks followed the rule of Saint Bernard. Among the tradesmen of the vicinity this rule had survived in various practices more or less faithful to its spirit. In her café, she said, the most recent of an unbroken line of bistros going back to the thirteenth century, the monkish rule was reflected in the custom Sir Joseph had seen enacted: a large glass of white wine mixed with red-currant liqueur was passed from one drinker to the next, each taking a swallow in turn until the glass was nearly empty, at which point it was either refilled or set aside. It was considered a kind

of sacrilege to drink the last of its contents as the Sardinian had un-
wittingly done.

Sir Joseph thanked the good-natured woman for the information and politely asked if her family's ownership of the café also originated in the middle ages. She shook her head, explaining that she
had acquired the lease only ten years before, at great expense: because of the famous tradition associated with it, the café, in spite of
its humble air, attracted the richest and most distinguished customers in that section of town. She had been able to pay the necessary
price only through her daughter's talent and affection. A coloratura
singer of great virtuosity, that young woman had one evening, at a
reception given by the Marquis de Batz, been challenged by Charles
Bergman, a wealthy diamond merchant and notorious gambler, to
sing Constanza's "Martern aller Arten" a whole tone higher than
written, offering against the unlikely exploit an eight-carat cut blue
diamond of perfect water. The singer said that she would accept the
challenge if the jeweler subsequently renewed his gage for each of
the four superior semitones. By the end of the evening she had performed the aria five times, ultimately reaching an unimaginable b-
flat above high c. Charles Bergman kept his word and thus gave the
daughter an opportunity to manifest her filial devotion: delivered on
the following day, the stones were then presented by the daughter to
her astonished mother, who refused all but one; advantageously sold,
it had brought her possession of the prestigious café.

When, comforted with a sandwich and another coffee, he went
out onto the street, Sir Joseph turned to the left. He at once realized
his mistake, sensing that it had been anything but fortuitous: it pointed
to an unconscious awareness on his part that he had entered a new
realm, that all his careful reckonings had been meant to lead him

here so that he could turn left on a narrow sidewalk in a drab street. He could now begin to see where he was. The new realm was the exact image, greatly reduced, of the one along which he had maneuvered through the day; within it surely was a yet smaller space, and that would be his next and final goal. The complementarity he had so hopelessly sought lay not beyond, but within. He started on his last lap, with an eagerness and anxiety so intense that to distract himself he, Sir Joseph Pernican, actually started whistling Constanza's air loudly as he walked.

VIII

As he turned right off the thoroughfare onto a narrow street that bore slightly to the left and whose far end he could not clearly distinguish, Sir Joseph was anything but surprised to discover where his final destination lay. The little street was charming, although he could not immediately tell why. To the left were conventional middle-class apartment buildings, to the right older and smaller houses with nondescript façades and treeless courtyards behind them visible through occasional gratings. All too soon he realized what sensation had agreeably overcome him — it was a sensation of familiarity — and as he did so it soured into a kind of despair. He had been mercilessly trapped

The street ended not in the narrow angle he expected but in an L-shaped turn to the left, and it was when he saw it that he knew exactly where he had arrived. On the third floor of one of the small old houses, thirty years before, he had lived — he had failed to live — the passion of his life. It had been a passion so furious he had been frightened by it, and after a few months he had abandoned his lover

She was a dancer; her body was small, supple, strong, and smooth; her own passion expressed itself with knowledgeable ardor. He had fled. More exactly, he had by his boorishness provoked her into making him flee. He had not pursued her, won her, abducted her from her house, or guarded her from the attentions of others; he had not had to relinquish her through any force of circumstance. He had followed her and lain down with her and her agile loins, then allowed himself through willful negligence to be sent away. Now, choking helplessly at this wildest of all deaths, covering his faculties in the black wax of night, he succumbed to a rage of remorse.

Some clambering vine, clematis or wisteria, sprawled among the windows of the housefront. He crossed the street and seized its thick stem in both hands, shaking it as if to wrench it from the wall and its diminutive plot of earth. Leaves and twigs rattled against mortared stones. She opened the window to see what was happening. She had aged very little. She did not recognize him, using the formal pronoun of address when she asked him what he was doing. He turned away without an answer and rounded the corner onto a busy, tree-lined avenue.

He paid no more attention to where he went. At last he came to a little park and sat down on one of its green benches. Grass had grown up unmown between plane trees and horse chestnuts past their flowering. He gazed stupidly in front of him.

Out of the grass a lark rose with singular verticality and speed high into the air, high above the trees, a stationary flutter in the afternoon sunlight.

Watching the bird, Sir Joseph shook his head, then laughed out loud. He stood up and walked out of the park, as he did so dropping his packet of documents into a trash can. He kept his map as souvenir, although he feared that neither then nor thereafter would he be able to say whether it was meant to recall the lark's sudden ascent or its golden hovering.

THE TAXIDERMIST

In the ring of her left index finger and thumb she gently tugged on the slender tubes.

"I can't stand it."

She was still as a Poussin priestess.

"Come *on*."

"It'll never be better."

"Yes yes it will."

"And then?" She slightly eased her left hand but kept hold of nothing else but mere tip. "And then?"

"Then the works. Please."

"Make it last?"

"I'll die."

"No sweeter way to go?"

"*Yes*."

"Mmm?"

"Oh, yes."

She opened his way with her right index and medius, holding his thighs fast under her shins. A dip; a tuck; a relaxed space for the notion of spontaneous self-expression; a firm and gentle nip. If not beautiful, his clenched hissing face looked sincere enough.

Eventually she tipped up the flag of the antique taxi meter on her bedside table. She ran this curio in remembrance of a childhood ride in a Checker, when she'd knelt frontwards on a jumpseat and watched the driver play pocket pool at red lights. (For her own trips, she charged a flat rate.)

SOAP OPERA

for Lynn Crawford

At a distance, the backlit object resembles a decorative tabletop gadget, one that must be upended to allow its load of small pellets to start cascading, through a liquid as transparent and dense as shower gel, down an arrangement of slides, spiral grooves, or more complex detours. Here the arrangement is that of a beehive, in which each hexagonal cell allows passage through at least one, usually two, and sometimes three of its walls. Emanating from a hidden source, the pellets, already discernible at a distance as hollow rings, flood into the hive from above and slowly make their way through the layers of cells (seventy-three in all), following courses that vary from broken but essentially straight downward lines to elaborate, irregular paths that may lead, for example, from one edge of the hive to the other and back. Whatever its trajectory, each ring eventually drops from the bottom of the hive into the obscurity below, an obscurity no less impenetrable than that from which the ring first emerged. The variability of the paths is due to the unforeseeable speed and angle with which a ring may strike the side of a cell or another ring, as well as by the erratic accessibility of the aperture through which it will pass into the next cell.

As the viewer approaches the construction, it becomes apparent that something relatively small occupies the hollow of each ring. A still closer view reveals that these presences, from afar seen as no more than specks, are in fact featherless bipeds. The rings, it turns out, are not properly rings at all, since each has a depth at least twice as great as its diameter: they are large cylinders, rather like truncated sections of pipeline. The bipeds inside them seem at home in their mobile and indeed unstable habitats. They adapt nimbly and naturally to the turnings of the cylinders and the shocks occasioned by frequent collisions. They can clearly distinguish between bouncing off a cell wall and encountering another cylinder. Such encounters evidently inspire them with rejoicing or intense anxiety, according to their temperaments or perhaps earlier experiences, and provoke in the great majority of cases a flurry of activity specifically designed to make their reactions known to those whose paths they happen to have crossed: tapping or pounding with their forearms against the cylinder walls, rhythmic jumping or thumping with their feet, and some kind of articulate falsetto shrieking (at least that is what an observer deprived of direct acoustical evidence visually deduces it to be). Frequently two (sometimes more than two) cylinders will be not only brought but kept together by chance, so that they share a common path during the next stage of their journeying. In most instances this generally prompts initial signs of tremendous satisfaction in one or both of the bipeds whose shells are thus attached, although more often than not these signs of satisfaction tend to disappear after a certain time. Be that as it may, sooner or later a difference in the angle of rebounding, or a collision affecting one cylinder and not the other, separates the two. Each inmate then, as before, concentrates exclusively on directing the course of its cylinder's progress.

For such, indeed, is what each unmistakably thinks it is doing: by positioning itself in a certain part of the cylinder, or by moving up and down its inner surface in a deliberate manner, or even by performing virtually stationary actions that are mechanically incomprehensible but may serve some propitiatory function, it is expressing a conscious determination to control its itinerary through a maze whose disposition remains beyond its sight and ken, as well as through a host of similar moving objects whose very presence can be determined only haphazardly. Most cylinder inmates nevertheless exhibit extraordinary and lasting confidence in this power to direct their own way; and their confidence might be justified—all viewers have observed examples of prowess in reacting to collisions and even, somehow, in anticipating them—if the openings in the cell walls were arranged according to a pattern. Since in this respect great care seems to have been taken to avoid all regularity, the results achieved by even the finest maneuvers remain illusory beyond any but the briefest of spans.

In time the strenuousness of the exertions required by this never-ending struggle for navigational mastery tires out the bipeds who inhabit the cylinders. Before their containers have tumbled out of the lowest rank of cells, most have abandoned their efforts or at least decided—and none but the coldest-hearted observer will fail to sympathize with them—that the time has come for a well-deserved rest. It is in this attitude of exhaustion or repose that we watch them disappear from view. Some, it is true, labor to the end with an energy that cannot readily be interpreted as manifesting either enthusiasm or despair. It remains impossible to judge whether their ultimate fate merits such an expense, or whether it differs from that of their quieter brethren to any significant degree. Most likely this notion belongs to the domain of pathetic fallacy rather than to that of true possibilities, by which I mean those that a scrupulous observer might reasonably entertain.

JOURNEYS TO SIX LANDS

1

Out of droning Bayonne at five, sun silhouetting a Buddha on the city's one shrine. We had fashioned a mast for our hull from a stout pine that we felled and lopped in the dark, amid much blasphemy. By lantern light we saw what some nimble climber had long ago carved in its fork, "*I* before *he* except after *she*" — weird words leading to argument over what they might portend. Once the mast was stepped and braced with stays, we raised our sails with halyards we had braided out of rawhide. There is a tear in the leech of our mainsail. We glided down the river between zones of industrial waste. Only a few indifferent gulls watched us leave. It is after all a poor, deserted place. Tiers of mussels ringed the pilings of abandoned wharves in the lowering tide. There is an inexplicable tear in the leech of the mainsail. We were bound for home — a home that we had forgotten or never seen.

2

Standing away north from the coast, the wind sitting east-northeast
a harsh quarter — we could do nothing but drive, scudding away a
we bore against it, mast sloping, bow dipping. We had no true offic
ers but encouraged each other to stand to the tackle, stretch on th
oars, contract the luffing sails, everything a struggle, with the se
swirling and hawling inboard, in a shrilling of stays and halyards. W
forgot the new old world we longed for. We had taken a priest name
Dory on board; he now passed among us, intoning the opening word
of the fifty-first psalm and raising crossed sticks over each of us as h
did so in a kind of infernal blessing. Such a handsome man, young
light-hearted, not a drowning mark on him, master of men and o
women, too! He was to enrapture all our loveliest in turn. Even now
in those endragoned seas, he took Dominique into the dark belov
the leaking cabin decking. At one moment the waves rose from such
a depth I saw the floor of the sea: lobsters five feet long and scurryin
crabs with glowing eyes. Later, the sky seemed boundless, full of fierc
stars.

3

We drifted into a stinking fog, thick with what felt like soot. The killer-squalls had passed on — one man and a boy washed overboard. The mainsail was tattered; half the snap hooks on the jib would not close; all our circuits were broken. The sails for now were of no use anyway: not a breath of wind. We worked hard at our oars though with heavy hearts, like men going to execution. (It seems our sweat made the ladies hot — it was Gloria's impatient turn with Dory today.) The water was laden with ooze, with something like clay. We dreaded running aground in the dark. Next to the steersman, whose face gleamed white by his lamp, a woman sat holding a frond wetted with vinegar, to slap him in case he nodded off. I looked up once and there stood the cook in his greasy girdle, not a sign of care on his filthy-bearded face as he shucked a bucket of mussels, tossing shells over our heads into the sad water. The place and time of our embarcation were already beyond any wish to remember them.

4

Was there a droning in the fog? The smell had gotten worse. Afraid that the splashed water was toxic, some rowers wore soul-and-body lashings in spite of the heat. We came among quiet, turgid eddies and a sudden voluminous cloud of night-flying white moths: land nearby? "In that case," someone said, "it must be the land beyond the sun." A pier emerged from the darkness, protruding from an acre of barren ground. At its tip three figures were imploring to be taken on board. Dory and Faith, his day's companion, helped each over the gunwale with a finger entwined in his hair. As we moved off, rowing still (first our propellors had fouled, now the throttle cable stuck), we felt a solid thing hindering our progress. Someone recognized the body of our lost boy. When we leaned over to recover him, the cook, nibbling a dish of goose lungs as he spoke, said flatly that he would not have him aboard. He picked up an abandoned oar and pushed him under, easy enough with his garments so heavy with the drink. Poisonous or not, these waters provide no fish. We live on fowl salted or smoked.

5

We entered a cluttered expanse, without tide or current, full of indistinct shoals that diminished our passageway (but with no sign of a shore to set foot on). The fog's darkness was speckled with local lights. They emanated from isolated erections and wrecks that rose out of the slick water. On them men and women, alone or in groups of two and three, sat in the glow of lanterns, candles, battery lamps, even flashlights. Some called to us as we passed. On one stout pile a pretty girl stood reading; she looked up when we were close by and imperturbably announced, *"The Bled and the Rack."* A young couple kept singing "Three blind mice" backwards, over and over, perched on a half submerged oil derrick. From the upended stern of a hulk, where he was arguing violently with a middle-aged man in orange djellabah and dark glasses, a pimply adolescent shouted, "Can anyone straighten out the fucking Trinity for us?" (Dory made as if to reply, remembered that Agnes was waiting, and turned away.) With the warnings from the bow lookout, these voices kept the air crackling with staccato speech. A dozen mergansers with bright-patched wings floated out of our way. The backs of fat slow eels heaved on the oily surface. We abandoned all thought of a fixed destination, hoping at best to avoid circling through this region of stench and gloom. The garboard seams had started leaking.

6

Borne by a mild current that glided due north, we emerged from the fog into clear red light. We scanned the heavens to see if the sky itself was red, but there was no sky to be seen, only uniform red brightness. It revealed the sorry state of our ship — the planks warped, several ribs cracked; there was no health in it. Soon the current started changing directions in complex, unpredictable ways. At first the lakelike surface was empty, even of rolling fish, but in time we began seeing occasional swimmers. At last a barge-sized wherry appeared, Venetian in aspect, with its black lacquer and gold trim. It was manned by a crew of young men in blue-and-white striped denims. When the cook came on deck and spotted them he exclaimed, "That's where I belong!," at once calling out "Hard a lea!," *the* most foolish of commands, since there was no wind at all; furthermore, we would never let him go. We told him as much. Then the cook in a rage laid hold of Dory and threw him over the side. The young man stupidly floundered out of reach, to be eventually fished up by the barge's hands, although they held him firmly under water for a minute before taking him aboard. Holly was grief-stricken, Jeannette saddened that her turn would now never come.

7

"… wandering around a place like this when the far shore appears. We aren't expecting it. It's just after dawn — I notice a couple of hills way off, almost black against the light. As we get closer I can see a meadow sloping down to the edge of the water. It's covered with red and yellow flowers, maybe ankle-high. There's a breeze blowing from the land, the kind that comes off snow when it's melting. The sun is up. The air's *shining*. We hear a quiet tune from somewhere in the woods past the meadow. The east is turning bright pink and the sky is still dark blue when a woman walks out of the woods. She's wearing a green cape with a day-glo orange robe underneath. At first her face is in shadows — 'a veil of leafy flowers' — but even when she's standing in sunlight down by the water we can't really make her out. There's no way we can get close enough in, too shallow, with masses of rotting seaweed. Anyway no one is seriously thinking of going ashore. It's too much; as if nothing we ever did matters any more. And the song — I can't remember a note of it now. You know how it is. Something like 'Little Buttercup,' if you've ever heard that."

8

The garboards went in a new fog, against a smother of sand. It may take us a thousand years to get over it, drinking Clos Vougeot *déclassé* with our easygoing likenesses, stubbornly soaking our cares and years, always remembering that as long as you keep swallowing any thought of suffocation can be dispelled. What probably irks most is the prospect that, after all this nonsense, we may some day again put on fleshly raiment. But for the moment this seems a remote possibility. Hats, pencils, two unmatched shoes, and a few suited bodies go drifting by, tossed by the oven-hot wind blowing off the western verge, sometimes sticking in massed tangles of weed. The tar on old boards that have settled against the banks has blistered in the sun. Small eels cluster in warmer shallows; gaping mussels slope down the mud onto the slimy flats, where crabs scuttle sidelong in inch-deep water. A long-forgotten oil lamp, rusted and shattered, has sunk halfway into the purple ooze. This is Cythera, lady.

9

Out of droning fog the broad river quietly flowed due north between dry wastes, with no light from the cold sky but the moon's. It had passed us by. It is an understatement to say that our mast and bow no longer sloped or dipped, that our pumps had clogged and our chain plates rusted: we were as inert as what can be depicted in solid coloring when applied to suitable material (durable or not—belly of vase or square of cloth): a vessel resting on an immensity of water similarly depicted (see below). As the river moved on, clayey shoals had begun hindering its progress, damming and dividing its currents. Fragmented, diminished, unburdened, its streams pressed their way between sandbanks and islands matted with reeds, along riversides where tight-lipped mussels blacker than the night declined into the slow water; until in time a sound of breaking waves announced its destination, which at last opened in front of it unbounded, glittering with the light of freshened stars.

CLOCKING THE WORLD ON CUE:
THE CHRONOGRAM FOR 2001

NOTE: The chronogram — a centuries-old literary form — follows a simple but demanding rule: when all letters corresponding to Roman numerals (*c, d, i, l, m, v,* and *x*) are added together, they produce a sum equivalent to a specific year of the Christian calendar. The single words *memory* and *memento* are thus chronograms of the year 2000 (*m* x 2); so are *A moment for feasts & prayers* (*m* x 2) and *A year to pay homage to the dead* (*m* x 1 + *d* x 2). Both the title and text of this work are examples of chronograms of the current year.

January starts: sun here, stars there. So what joys & fears has the New Year brought us?

• In the Irkukst penitentiary ironworks the night shift is finishing its stint, skirting weighty pig-iron ingots as it regains the prison interior.

• In Pienza, Ernestina is heating tripe *fiorentina* for thirteen.

• In Sing-Sing, wearing surreptitious attire, spiting the surprising North Irish negotiations & shrinking tensions, Phineas, retiring Bishop of Ossining, with the authorities' requisite inattention, is tonight anointing fifteen Fenian ("Fighting Irish") priests in a rite of injurious piety.

- Bibi is shirring pigeon eggs in Saint Étienne.

- In Brighton, gregarious Brother Ignatius is getting high quaffing his fifth straight Irish whisky.

- In Pretoria, gritty Erwin Higginson (age eight), ignoring fatigue & injuries, is winning his point in a bruising nineteen-eighteen tiebreaker against Fritz Spitzfinger (age nine) by returning a wristy spinner hip-high & without hesitation whipping it fair, Spitzfinger then batting it high into the rows to bring the fifteenth prestigious Witherspoon Tennis Initiation Tourney to a breathtaking finish.

- In Fuji, pursuing a hashish high with Quentin, Kenny is perusing sporting prints by Hiroshige & Hokusai.

- Arising at eight in Brisbane, Ian, aspiring historian of propitious intuitions, enjoys the benign aberration that, by getting a grip on his utopian fusion of Augustinian with Einsteinian reasoning, he is attaining a genuine gnosis.

- In Etrurian Tarquinia, Gigi is eating spaghetti with pepperoni

- In Austria, zipping past the Inn, ignoring warning signs, Pippo Peruzzi, first-string Ferrari whiz, big winner in Spain & Argentina, is steering his touring bike (pistons & turbine whirring, its stunning furnishings genuine Pinin-Farina) in brisk pursuit of fiery Zizi, his Hungarian skier, itinerant antithesis, antagonist, tigress, priestess, siren, obsession, happiness, wife.

- Bobbie is sitting with Bert in a Parisian bistro, in whose noisy interior untiring opportunists are satisfying pretentious ninnies with inferior white wine.

- Heroin originating in Iquitos is winning first prize with tertiary bargaining arbitrators in Tijuana.

- Bonnie is frying onion rings in Triffin (Ohio).

- In antique Poitiers, Antoinette is refreshing her guests with interpretations of Rossini's quainter offerings, interspersing arias & ariettas with his *"Nizza"* (singer & piano), his *"Raisins"* & *"Noisettes"* (piano), his first *sinfonia* (strings), & his roguish *"Iphigénie"* (bass trio).

• In Tirana, inept Hussein is paying fifty-eight qintars to fortify his Istrian wine with Bosnian raki.

• In the wintry outskirts of Pori, Father Tiki Haakinen — enterprising & itinerant Finnish priest — is repairing hi-fi wiring for a parish benefit.

• In spite of its threat to her ingratiating Gibson waist, Rikki, in Zanzibar, is insisting on heaping & eating piggish portions of spaghetti & fig pie.

• Postponing inopportune issues & putting first things first, Kiwanis, Rotarians, & Shriners are putting their agonizing unity in writing, signing a proposition that reasserts their opposition to atheists, bigotry, euthanasia ("outright assassination"), heroin, pinkos, the Spanish Inquisition, superstition, & unfairness in business arbitration.

• Fate, or perhaps the outrage of one hurt spirit, separates father & son for many years of harsh regret.

• In Antibes, binging on *pastis* is getting Winnie higher than nine kites.

• In Kiruna, in white tie, sipping a Perrier, Fafnir Grieg, high priest of Ibsen initiates, is testing his register & intonation in painstaking preparation for his fiftieth signature interpretation of the protagonist in *Ghosts*.

• In Gorizia, Anita is working up an appetite for *anitra triestina* roning sheets.

• At Trinity, Robin is boating with his tutor, Isaiah Singe. Isaiah s asking if Robin thinks he is going to finish his thesis *(Affinities with the Orient: Inquiries into spurious interpretations of Hafiz in Ariosto, Ossian & Kropotkin)* within his transitory span of years.

• In Bingen, penurious Winston is spiking his uninspiring Pepsi with Steinhäger.

• Business-wise Erika O'Higgins is sitting in Pittsburgh squinting with attention at the infuriating fine print in an IRS opinion assigning Irish pension benefits she is repatriating. The opinion questions her attestation separating foreign benefits, earnings as insurer in Tangier & those in fringe proprietary rights in Eritrea; pinpoints gains transpiring through inquiries into unwritten but propitious negotiations in Haiti; & reinstates profits inherent in eight-figure operations she is authorizing in Bisk (Siberia).

• In Bonaire (Georgia), hungry Josiah is weighing into his piping-hot grits & grunts.

• Rehearsing *Rienzi* in her Gorki isba, Anastasia thinks of Patti singing in *I Puritani*, of Kipnis in *Boris*, of Kiri Te Kanawa's Rosina in a Göttingen *Figaro*.

• In Ostia, engaging Ethiopian waiters trigger big tips by squirting nips of *grappa* into porringers of out-of-season fruit.

• Batting against the Orizaba Tigres in Irapuato, rookie Juanito Arias first whiffs in eight straight opportunities before hitting a ninth-inning zinger & satisfying the inhabitants' hopes of winning the Zapatista Series.

• Zazie is biting into rabbit thighs in Barbizon.

• Zenia, passionate Aquinist, is pursuing an ingenious hypothesis, assigning the origins of Aquinas's interpretations of Gorgias to an "Osirian" genesis arising in the writings of inquiring Egyptian priests, an origin that the Sophists reinstate, or so Zenia infers in her ingenious synthesis. Questioning the suppositions of post-Aquinist thinkers, Zenia insists on the inferiority of Fourier's "inanities," Wittgenstein's "gibberish," & Austin's "asininities."

- High-intensity spirits inspire high-intensity spirit in noisy Kirin.

- In an uninspiring quarter of Trier, Ohioan Josiah, a boisterous nineteen, is infuriating Swiss Inge, a serious thirty, by persisting in attributing the first apprehension of the Einstein shift to Igor Sikorsky.

- In a *ristorante* in Torino, sheepish Antonio's superstitious hesitation between *arrabiata* spaghetti & risotto with *funghi* both intrigues & irritates patient Giorgina.

- In Ottawa, thirteen Inuit Situationists are signing treaties with the nation's highest authorities guaranteeing that their tribes & regions inherit proprietary herring-fishing rights outright & in perpetuity.

- In Whitby, seagoing Einar, finishing his fifteenth pink gin, insists he is quite fine.

- In Twinsburg (Ohio), when a nitwit intern, threatening to irrigate her intestines with his "own unique quinine infusion," brings out a giant syringe, Queenie, a patient with hepatitis B, her weary inertia shattering at the threat of this aggression, begins reiterating in shrieks of irritation & anguish, "No penetration without representation!"

- Ski-touring in Bennington, Jiri spits out bits of unripe kiwi in a fit of pique.

- Supine in Biarritz, Tristan — unsparing onanist — is perusing Gautier's pornographies, whose swift prurient inspiration stiffens his waning spirits.

- In Rosario (Argentina), fiery Antonio is assuaging his thirst with sweetish Rhine wine.

- Ianthe, in Berkshire, is initiating with requisite ingenuity her inquiry into "Oppositions & affinities in the autobiographies of Gibbon, Twain, & Frank Harris."

• In the Ain, Fifi is eating pike patties.

• In their frigate-repair station in Hawaii, engineer's assistant Rossetti is preparing to assassinate his superior, Ensign Fink, for gratuitous insinuations about his inferior IQ.

• Anisette fizzes are winning the night in Springs, whither Henri is steering Bettina in his antique Hispano-Suiza.

• Rehearsing Griffith's reinterpretation of the *Oresteia*, Saint Rita is pursuing Sinatra — a horrifying Aegistheus — then knifing Frank in his upstairs bathing unit. Arguing about the Patripassian & Arian heresies, Ignatius, Athanasius, & Boethius irritate an otherwise patient Hypatia. Portia is propositioning Iago. Tweetie, Isaiah, & Sophie Goering are intoning Britten's (or is it Griffin's?) "Fair Oriana." With Thisbe furnishing her know-how to position the pair, King Henry the Fifth is trying to insert his uninteresting penis into a twittering Titania. The White Rabbit appraises Pippa passing with irony and pity.

• In Saint-Quentin, Pierre is into his fifth pinkish Pinot Noir.

• Writing *finis* to his reign in the prize ring in Ashanti, Nigeria, "Tiger" Titus (Niger) is forfeiting a bruising fist fight to his Ibo heir, Tobias, thus ratifying his apparent superiority.

• In a quaint inn in Rieti, Kiki & Brigitte sniff quasi-appetizing brain fritters hissing in swine fat.

• Fishing in Touraine, Irwin is unkinking Eugenia's rig & fitting it with spinners. Their skiff sits in a quiet bight where feisty, spiky pike are rising & biting. First strike! It is raining.

• Uriah, Iggi, Jennifer, Tabitha are hitting the Pinot Grigio in a wine bar in Waikiki.

• In Fife, Inigo Higgins finishes writing his iniquitous *Jottings on Kinship Etiquette in Barrie, Rattigan, Braine, & Pinter.*

• Gauging his position in the whitening Pakistanian heights, Piotr eats his fiftieth fig out of its tin.

• Its gregarious parties gathering at a transient staging-point, shipping in the Bering Straits, either freight or passenger, is stationary tonight — engines quiet, neither jib nor spinaker astir. As the fortieth ship nears, persistent skiffs begin sprinting through the nippy waters, swapping ostentatious rations & surprising potations & ferrying a rotation of seafaring prostitutes out of Tientsin, Biak, Iquique, Teresina, Kauai, Tenerife, Piraeus, & Hoboken.

• In Whitefriars, Pip infers that he is gaining genuine insights by sharing a firkin of Guinness with Brian.

• In Perugia, unwise Arrigo Panin is preparing a presentation hat, straining notions of affinities to their breaking-point, risks irking (or boring) knowing trainees in his Institute for Insight & Orientation by arguing that it is appropriate to attribute Hopkins's inspiration to Whittier, Stein's to Browning.

• Faith is refrigerating nineteen stingers & braising nine satiating portions of bison brisket in Topperish (Washington).

• Hiking in the interior of Shikoku, Kirk is sustaining a tiring Iris with aspirins & interesting attributions of Finnegan's epiphanies.

• Sophie & Étienne, in an Iberian setting, are swigging refreshing pints of sangria *gratis.*

• In Sabine, righteous Sheriff Winthrop Prior, feinting a right, is banging a furious fist into a hirsute rapist's ribs & a punishing thigh into his iniquitous groin.

• Georgianna is nourishing nine aging kittens in Big Sur.

• Benign skies in Arizona. At a prairie spring, Tintin is watering his proprietor's thirty-eight first-string ponies — they're skittish ponies, stirring, neighing, biting, nosing bitten withers. Rising high in his stirrups, reins tight against bit, quirt hanging at his wrist, Tintin spits; sitting, he tips a sparing ration into its Zigzag wrapping. Prairie rabbits thinking: rain. Harriers beating their wings in thin bright air. Tintin thinking: this night's attire — white shirt, string tie — is right for winning his engaging señorita. His pinto whinnies & pisses.

• Sipping saki in Gifu, Roshi is getting quite tipsy.

• Zigzagging in nifty figure eights on a skating rink in frosty Keewatin, Nettie is fantasizing an ingenious haikuisation of Swinburne's "Proserpine."

• In Pistoia, tiny Pierino, stripping a thin bit of appetizing skin off the shining ribs of a spit-roasting pig, bites into it with a grin.

• Within sight of eternity, Keith Asquith, wintering in Antigua, is taking unsparing pains to surprise, spite, & punish his nowise ingratiating Yorkshire heirs — "The shits!"

• In Iowa abstainers are abstaining.

• In Austin, Ira & Justina, a striking pair, registering at first sight no antipathies but intriguing affinities, wishing to kiss, interiorize their inhibitions, banish their hesitations, skip propositions, & kiss, hip against hip. A swift shifting into a pertinent interior to quit their attire: whipping off pigskin trainers, unbuttoning Ira's shirt, stripping off Justina's T-shirt, unzipping her tight-fitting skirt & his khakis, unhooking her brassiere, ripping away panties & briefs, ignoring trinkets, skin to skin. . . . "Wait," interrupts Justina, insisting, "first this joint," to forthwith initiate brisk intakes & an instantaneous high. Kissing again, Ira's fingertips graze with finesse Justina's hair, ribs, & thighs. Justina seizes his wrists & entwines his waist between jittering tibias. Straining, Ira nips her tits. Thrashing, her nips stiffening,

Justina tightens her grip. Gratifying Justina's appetite for kissing with ingenious bites, in his benign yearning Ira using his weight tips her posterior hither, baring Justina's piping fig. Into this engaging shrine Ira insinuates his inspissating thing, an insertion that ingratiates writhing Justina, inquiring in its penetration of her gripping, shifting pith, whose stunning twinges infuse Ira with stinging fire. He begins panting, his sinews stiffen, he hisses, Justina shrieks. It's brief, it's nifty, it's insane. Supine & sweating, Ira & Justina sigh faint sighs, kiss, grin, & sink into unworrying, transitory night.

• In the Tsinking zoo, unhesitating hippos, giraffes, kiwis, penguins, tortoises, porpoises, & tigers are ingesting big propitiatory portions of grain, onions, fruit, ginger, fish, & pig.

• On Thirteenth Street & First, Antoine & Honoria are sharing a pizza & a knish.

• Aries & Sirius are shining in Tunisian skies,

& so our New Year has begun.

ONE-WAY MIRROR

for Francesco Clemente

Of the sixteen ways of getting there, she recommended the Upper India Express departing from Tundla Junction at twenty past 2 A.M., arrival 6:15, first and air-conditioned second class, dining car, supplement payable.

But from here? What about from here?

Soon after his arrival, he had adopted a little dog. It and its own tawdry retinue of house crows, which waddled behind it while it sniffed out treasures of half-hidden refuse. In return they raucously guarded it from larger curs. When a local cook offered to buy this overweight mongrel, he explained that the puppy's name meant God.

He saw an advertisement about a mirror that took forty photographs per minute as soon as it was activated by a moving object. (He had thought: moths and spiders; razor grimaces; someone narcissistically jerking off.) Later, when he mentioned it to her, she was reminded of a sound-activated tape recorder she'd heard about. It was sold with an inaccessible password. A red on-light and the clicking of the cassette testified to its apparent operation, otherwise taken on trust. The point: "It was an incorruptible witness of our words, the nearest thing to God on the market. Whenever you speak, you know that you are known."

He first saw her on the beach in early, still bearable sun. Languidly painting a list of titles on a shanty wall: *The Awkward Screw. The Turn of the Carpet. What Daisy Knew* . . . He stopped to watch. She said to him, "He was our Golden Ass." Inside the squalid shack, he picked up a discarded square of stamped metal whose surface was bright but mat and stared into its glow, his eye straining to read the unreflecting blur. She showed him a rug in whose corners the evangelists appeared as fleshless heads, with variants of their attributes aligned diagonally away from them: money bag and Dictaphone; turpentine bottle and yogurt jar; an animal fang; a feather — the rest were threadbare. The diagonals met at a circle enclosing a cartoon face of Queen Victoria.

He met her again in the evening. She wore a sari made of fine starched net on which Chopin's E minor Prelude had been finely inscribed, so draped, he staringly noticed, that its climax, with an eighth-note high C sharp at the apex, fitted the veiled interstice of her reins.

He saw her as often as she allowed. A trivial illness had tired him. He said to her, "Syringe needles, enema nozzles, jaws of leeches, all the tools of medicinal withdrawal hunt us down in order to void us, and not just of the filth we're supposedly hiding." He could see Byron's doctors bleeding him to death. She replied: "You are being simple-minded. A remedy truly described is more like a sibylline paradox than a prescription. Needles are two-way. So is a pen: it does nothing but leak ink, and at the same time you speak to it, attending to its thirst with letters and syllables, nourishing its demands with everything you've forgotten. The pen sits on your lap waiting like a bung with its hinged stopper to draw out something to be tasted. The pen is your nose and your spine. It's the tree of the knowledge of ignorance. It's what you are stuck with; face it. This is being not simple-minded, provided you remember that there are two nostrils to your nose and that your tail is cleft. I acknowledge that your wearing a fern as a necktie adds to your attractiveness, but I must point out that you plainly intend it to signify a mouse-like innocence that you never had. You will not lose by letting it go. Let the ink dry, read it later." He shit.

Each meeting withdrew the green baize curtain separating him from air and light, only to reveal another expanse of baize plunged in shadows that made the designs on it hopelessly pertinent and ob-scure. She covered his eyelids and lips. She let his penis grow into a tree.

Rakan, that arrant proselytizer, came through the village scat-tering a pittance of coins to groveling kids, from whom he kept at a careful distance. They weren't kids at all but stunted, aging beggars. There was a panel discussion of the event. He defended Rakan. It was her doing. She told him, "Grease those beggars. Make them your runners. Have welcoming and farewell crowds wherever you go. It won't cost you a song." He asked the beggars for other references.

She would never pass him her joint or let him refill his wine glass until he had found a new, vivid metaphor of his desire (e.g. cormorant beak as it shakes a thrashing silver eel. Or, when she spurned him: to find — on that desolate island of jagged hills and unbearable summers with no life but a few *Kunar* trees, melon patches, and dust colored gazelles — the last melon). He explained that he never lisped as a child, but that at twelve corrective wires had been installed on his upper and lower front teeth that were unintentionally magnetized so that, if he closed his mouth, his jaws locked; for a brief time he lived open-mouthed and slept with a strip of insulating tape between his incisors.

Can the Ethiopian change his skin, or the leopard his spots? he asked, pronouncing it the way his mother used to, as if it were French. Yes, she answered, and told a tale of exploration that had taken her across the far east. Like many of her generation, she longed for spiritual enlightenment, which she hoped to attain through a transformation of sexual into psychic energy. Unlike many, she thought that such transformation would not be possible until her own sexual energy had ripened; she had never experienced full satisfaction of her preoccupying but wobbly desire. Because western doctors, psychotherapists, and counselors, all clitorally obsessed, only exacerbated her frustration, she turned for counsel to the worldly sages of distant cultures, traveling as far as Kyoto, Pushkar, even Luang Prabang. She often came away with profitable insights, but none of them helped her approach her goal. She was on the verge of giving up when, in the purlieus of the Mandalayan deminonde, she met a cheerful wizard who told her that he knew of one person who could help her, a woman living in the northern Shan States. She was tired of travel, but when he surprised her with an entrancingly reedy rendition of "Somewhere over the Rainbow," she accepted his advice. She laboriously journeyed to the capital of north Hsenwi (or Thienni) and for three weeks was there subjected several hours each day to the manipulations — intimate, indefatigable, and appallingly unhygienic — of a young woman with hands capable of steely strength and feathery delicacy. To the accompaniment of an interminable and, to her, incomprehensible keen, those hands touched, stroked, prodded, struck, stretched, and twisted every accessible point of her frightened, then submissive body. It was at the beginning of the second week, when the woman's left forefinger was pressing back her folded tongue and her right hand was crushing the toes of first one, then the other foot, that she at last understood and fully acquiesced in what was happening: by force, guile, or persuasion, the woman was teaching her physical self, half-inch by half-inch, to surrender every particularity of memory, expectation, and habit that encumbered it. She no longer endured their sessions but thrived on them. At their final meeting the young woman, undoing the braided mass of her black hair, cut from it a slender yard-long strand that, folded double, she thrust perhaps an inch into the anus of the now unflinching Irene (for that was her name), who was then bidden to put on her clothes before receiving a farewell blessing. During the ensuing weeks, brushing her inner thighs or pressed against them, Irene's hair tail chafed, tickled, and soothed her into a perpetual awareness of the young woman's powers. One day, while she was dancing a nostalgic Madison at an early-hours Bombay disco, the hair, swinging between her agile knees, brought on such an onslaught of desire that she knew that nothing could now scotch it. She went out into the dusk to a new lover and promptly achieved the gratification she had so long pursued.

He bit his tongue to keep from asking how. His own plans:

— Play her a tape whose sound, too low for the conscious ear, insinuated rumors of impending delight.

— Place the dried wishbone of the sacred *Anhinga* on her lips.

— Proceed according to local custom through the mediation of public scribes and advocates.

   — Appear by dark, coated in faintly luminous paints — red arms, blue legs, green genitals.

   — Run to her, down a path of pulsating red-gray coals.

   — Bring bliss to her mouth, a bowl of noodles reddened with his grandmother's long simmering sauce.

   — Caress her immediately but, as her account indicated, never nearing the focal bud of popular erotology even if, in another tale from her past, she had spoken of riding bareback as a young girl on a farm horse and nestling her nest against the bone of those hefty withers. (The Percheron had turned on her a right eye whose placid pupil was enclosed in a perfect circle and perfect sphere.)

   — While she slept, with the finest camel's hair brush speckle her body, starting at her soles, with enlivening dots of Andean cocaine.

   — Over many weeks touch her part by part, right ankle one day, ring finger the next, until the knot loosened.

By this time the air seemed to have grown hot enough for the sap in living wood to boil, damp enough for dead wood to resist ignition by blowtorch.

The first time took place late at night, simply and seriously, on the covered prow of a moored fishing bark, the *Yajnvalkya*.

The next time was accompanied by the staggered hour-long sequence of igniting incense-sparklers and cherry bomblets with which she had arrayed the six surfaces of the dark room.

The time after that brought a mutual constraint: a maximum duration of twenty-nine seconds.

The following time, endurance made him shut his eyes; when he opened them seconds later, she had disappeared from the house

The pre-pivotal time consisted of a classic Persian exercise known

s "The Two Forks." For instance, on the right-angled shelves he
aligned a cylinder of Triple-X film, a letter from his wife, a few pebbles
and shells, a bilingual copy of Owen Wister's *The Virginian,* resting his
head in the furred angle, eyes downward.

The pivotal time required that he buy her an electric blanket,
unheard of these climes (or any nearby). Before the week was out,
an express mail delivery from L.L. Bean caught her off her guard.
She then insisted they use it.

The post-pivotal time occurred somewhere between Ongole and
Kavali in a two-berth, air-conditioned-class compartment of the Grand
Trunk Express. The food was good. They arrived on schedule at 7 A.M.

The subsequent time, a screen separated them with, at one end,
symmetrically angled mirrors that allowed them to observe one another.

The antepenultimate time was set in a vacant lot by the weekly
market where, their work done, itinerant merchants ate, caroused,
and slept.

The next-to-last time was compellingly endured in the heat and
reek of blue-burning brimstone, of which several pots were littered
on the floor.

The last time, she told him he could do with her what he liked.
He requested permanence.

The heat intensified. He saw that feet or buttocks could not rest
unsquirming on any sunlit surface. When his dog curled up in a lee
of shadow, its members lay nicely detached from its body. One noon
he watched a lost moth light on a curl of strung iron wire to be heat-
sliced into perfect halves. He stared at untended dust kitties cluster-
ing into rhomboid patterns. There were no single flies, only swarms

as societal as grackles. Within him hummed a pullulation of verba
wrack; like "sling" endlessly recurring and evoking a defunct inter
national face (oriental, nameless); or repeated attempt to connec
the remembered Latin word for enemy with a forgotten Greek nam
for someone. He cursed the old school friend he saw waiting at th
bus stop. Let him stand in the punishing dust-paved sun until h
shriveled.

(The friend had arrived from Paris where, on an embankment o
the Seine, perhaps under the steamship hulk of the Ministry of Fi
nance, an invisible appointment had tipped him into fright, discol
oration, coughing, and dissolution, with no remedy other than com
pleting the process.)

She suggested as an alternative an earlier connection at Kanpa
Central Station, the Vaishali Express, departure ten past 1 A.M.
arrival 8:30, with similar accommodations (both trains operate i
the Northern Railway zone). In the Central and Western zone, th
best choice was the Dehra Dun Express from Bombay, leaving at 1
P.M., arriving at ten to 6 A.M.; no air conditioning, and no dining ca
with its little gray-blue paper bags of spice. She said she would loo
after his dog.

Whoever is elsewhere is wrong, even if the imagination can b
made real. He thought he remembered as much, the way the bird o
the bough remembers a cold-blooded past.

LANNAN SELECTIONS

The Lannan Foundation, located in Santa Fe, New Mexico, is a family foundation whose funding focuses on special cultural projects and ideas which promote and protect cultural freedom, diversity, and creativity.

The literary aspect of Lannan's cultural program supports the creation and presentation of exceptional English-language literature and develops a wider audience for poetry, fiction, and nonfiction.

Since 1990, the Lannan Foundation has supported Dalkey Archive Press projects in a variety of ways, including monetary support for authors, audience development programs, and direct funding for the publication of the Press's books.

In the year 2000, the Lannan Selections Series was established to promote both organizations' commitment to the highest expressions of literary creativity. The Foundation supports the publication of this series of books each year, and works closely with the Press to ensure that these books will reach as many readers as possible and achieve a permanent place in literature. Authors whose works have been published as Lannan Selections include: Ishmael Reed, Stanley Elkin, Ann Quin, Nicholas Mosley, William Eastlake, and David Antin, among others.